Redeemed Upon the Water

Lowlands Adventure Romance, Volume 2

Isabel Glover

Published by Isabel Glover, 2022.

REDEEMED UPON THE WATER

First edition. April 1, 2022.

ISBN: 979-8201326876

Written by Isabel Glover.

Also by Isabel Glover

Lowlands Adventure Romance
Hidden Beyond the Brae
Redeemed Upon the Water

Table of Contents

Chapter 1 - Isla

Isla Muir tried not looking the divers in the face as they exited the Eimear, but she smiled and said kind goodbyes as they all were her customers.

"Come back again," she forced out of her mouth, collecting any trash on the deck and putting it in a brown paper bag.

While most drivers were exhausted from the back-to-back dives, one man stayed behind, eager to talk more to Isla.

"Do you dive often?" the man asked, ready to step onto the dock his eyes watched as she cleaned.

Pausing, she glanced up at him. He had dark curly hair and a crooked tooth showed when he smiled. "No."

"Oh, well, you should try," he said, not getting the vibe that the ride was over, "There's amazing things that live down there."

"Uh-huh," Isla knew when creatures lived in the sea, and didn't need to be told the wonders of the water.

The space between the diver and Isla grew awkward.

"Would you be interested in dinner?" The diver asked, gesturing to the rooftops of the town with his thumb. "With me?"

"I'm married," Isla held up her right hand, which showed a thick band of silver.

"Oh, I'm sorry!" the man stumbled as he stepped off the boat and onto the dock. "I didn't realize, I didn't see the ring. Have a good day!"

Isla laughed as she watched him head to the dock house and around to the parking lot. With the trash collected, Isla organized the throw lines of the boat before heading to the boathouse. Logan, the dockmaster, sat inside at the front desk.

"Another successful trip?" The old man said, grinning up from his newspaper. His feet were crossed at the ankle and perched on his wooden desk. Below him was Tadg, the large Newfoundland that ruled the dock. The hound had perked an eye open to acknowledge the intruder, but seeing and smelling Isla, closed the glare and soon began snoring again.

"Always," Isla went to her locker, where she collected her belongings. Generally, she would take them with her, but not when she had a crowd on her boat. She didn't trust many travelers.

"That one straggler liked you," Logan still didn't look up from his newspaper, but all his attention was directed at the woman. "Did the ring work?"

"Not until I pointed it out," Isla pulled the silver band off and slipped it into her bag, sipping the pocket up. "He still fled like a rabbit."

"It isn't a perfect solution to suitors," Logan finally turned to look at her, "But it's something."

"Suitors," Isla laughed, shaking her head as she closed the door to her locker. "Your traditional ways."

"Gentleman callers?" Logan tried again, setting his newspaper down only to grab a drink from the glass resting on the desk. "You know, you could still—"

"I don't need a man, Logan," Isla interrupted him, but couldn't help but grin. She had a soft spot for the old man, as he had been her father's closest friend. "Except Tagh, maybe."

Hearing his name, the big dog jumped up from the floor and approached Isla. He licked her face a few times before returning to his spot by his master's feet.

"You need someone to help clean up the house," Logan's tone became serious, "And any man in town would be willing to help."

"I don't need help," Isla's smile vanished and she clutched her backpack tighter. "I'll see you tomorrow."

"Goodnight," Logan waved, picking the newspaper back up.

In the parking lot, Isla tossed her bag into the passenger seat of her pickup. The short drive to her father's house was filled with anxious energy. She hated going home, thinking about the piles of papers, documents, and hardcover books covering every surface of the interior dwelling. Light was blocked from the windows by the stacks on the wide window sills. Every table and chair was used as a bookshelf. The only surfaces free of clutter were the beds, the water closet, and the kitchen sink. When Isla first moved in, right after her father's death but before the funeral, she had to move two stacks of books from the dining room table and one chair to the floor so she had a place to sit and eat. Forget about holding a memorial or gathering there.

When she arrived home, Isla went straight to the kitchen and poured herself a bowl of cereal. She went right to her childhood bed and opened her laptop. While eating the multi-colored sugared carbs, she sorted through her email. A few service requests for the charter boat. A few spam emails. One email was from her university, from Anne.

"Hey Isla, hope you are doing well. I understand things have been rough for you, and we all here want you to take the time you need. But we also are worried about the experiments that still need to be run. Life happens, I know, but we need to know if you plan on coming back to continue your research. If you plan on taking more time, which is fine, we need to assign other technicians to your project. Let us know how you're doing, and if there's anything we can do for you. Best, Anne."

Isla's chest tightened as she read the email. The room seemed to shrink against her, and she found it difficult to breathe. When she had learned of her father's death two months ago, she had requested leave for a week to deal with arrangements. Her research team could hold the fort for a week. Then one week became two, and Isla found herself frozen in her duties. Her father's charter business continued as she accepted new gigs and customers. As much as she loved her salmon research on the east coast, she didn't know how to move on from her west coast hometown.

Opening the last email, Isla hoped it would distract her from her frantic state of mind.

"Hello Isla Muir,

This is Casper Shaw. I am letting you know I made it safely to town and will be able to drop off the deposit for the first dive trip tomorrow. Should I meet you at the dock to drop it off? Can't wait to get out on the water.

Best,

Casper Shaw."

When Isla first came in contact with Casper, she had thought he was reaching out to her for science purposes. Researcher to researcher. He said he was a marine biologist, like her, but worked on nudibranchs. While Isla enjoyed seeing colorful pictures of the sea slugs, she wasn't familiar with invertebrates. Even then, she was eager to help Casper. Then she realizes he was asking for a charter service, not for Isla's expertise specifically. Still, she was excited about the opportunity to work with a field researcher.

"Hi Casper,

Glad to know you arrived safely. I'll be doing boat maintenance on the dock tomorrow morning, so you can stop by then with the deposit. Just as Logan at the boathouse and he'll point you in the right direction.

See you then.

Isla Muir."

Reviewing the email, Isla scooped the remaining cereal from her bowl. The sugary solid loops dissolved on her tongue, and she remembered she needed to buy groceries. Another thing to add to the list, but her service provided meals for longer trips. Whatever she bought, the customer would have to eat. She wondered if Casper was a picky eater, and added a sentence to the email.

"Do you have any food preferences? I'm picking up supplies tomorrow for the trip."

Hitting send, Isla put her empty bowl to the side, closed her laptop, and laid her head down. She didn't feel like taking her dish down to the kitchen, where a mess of books waited on the counters.

Chapter 2 - Casper

Casper Shaw's heavy fingers buttoned up his flannel, leaving the top button undone. Then he pulled a heavy sweater over, pulling the collar out. The floor-length mirror reflected an image of a well-educated scientist who knows his shit, with a pair of new boat shoes peeking out from under the hem of his wrinkled khakis. He tried ironing out the creases from the long flight from New York City, but they wouldn't come out.

"Hi, I'm Casper Shaw," he rehearsed, looking himself in the eye, practicing a quirky grin, "I'm here from the UMASS Amherst to research nudibranchs in the Firth. Why? I love sea slugs, I think they're colorful, and their abilities to incorporate stinging cells into their physiology is wicked cool."

His grin faded, the feeling of failure reaching up inside his intestines and pulling at his emotional threads. At least he wasn't going to be working with another marine biologist. When he visited the website for Eimear Charter, he looked through the photo gallery. Pictures showed an older man, greying hair, with a few missing teeth standing on the hull of the Eimear, or talking to divers, or posing next to a young woman who shared similar facial characteristics as him. The "About Us" section didn't mention any degrees awarded from academic institutions, nor special training in the sciences, so the owner of the charter nor his daughter who was now running the business would see through Casper's charades.

Grabbing his wallet, Casper left the small cozy rental room and locked the door. As he walked down the narrow staircase, he could smell a breakfast smothered with butter and dairy. His stomach growled, and he looked at his watch. He had time before he had to go down to the docks.

"Bacon's almost ready, dear," said Mary, the owner of the house. She was a round woman with dark hair, but streaks of silver woven through her waves. The table was made with a white tablecloth with pink and green designs on the border, and it stretched down and almost touched the cushion seats of the neatly arranged wooden chairs. Platters of various sizes were set across the top, and all were overflowing with edible items. Biscuits, boiled eggs, fried eggs, scones, toast, and sausage links. A teapot rested in the middle, surrounded by delicate cups that fit in Casper's palm.

"You're up early," Mary said, finding a spot on the already-crowded table for the bacon, "Is your trip today, then?"

"No, no," Casper smiled, choosing a seat at the table with his back against the wall, "I'm still staying tonight and leaving tomorrow, but I have to get supplies ready today."

"Exciting what you do out there," Mary began fixing a pot of coffee, "Going out under the waves. I could never swim out past my knees, even when I was a child. The dark water always terrified me."

"When I first started diving," Casper said as he filled his plate with a little bit of everything, "I was scared of how dark everything was. In the Bahamas, the water is so clear and warm that you forget how deep you are. But in the north, the water gets dark quickly."

"You have flashlights, correct?"

"Uh-huh," Casper murmured as he shoved buttered toast into his mouth. "Very bright lights."

Setting the coffee pot on the table, Mary turned to the long kitchen counter and began washing dishes. Casper watched as he devoured the greasy meal, wondering if the old woman never stopped moving. He noticed that about women, they were always working, always fidgeting. His own mother had been like that at home or when he was in school, always making meals, cleaning, planning. His sister was also like that... before she died.

The thoughts of Bella crept into Casper's mind, so to distract himself, he poured himself a mug of coffee and drank it black. The bitter hot liquid washed down the crumbs from his teeth, and almost burned his esophagus. He coughed a little, but at least he was no longer thinking of the past.

"I'll be back this afternoon," he told Mary, out of courtesy.

"Enjoy yourself, dearie," Mary said, not turning from the running sink.

The cute coastal town was something out of a British Countryside calendar or a fancy baking show, with paved roads absent of potholes, sidewalks fashioned with cobblestones, and historical stone buildings built five hundred years prior. The cemetery by the church had gravestones that were no longer legible but records showed ancestors from before the American Revolution. Casper remembered in his own country seeing gravestones of Founding Fathers, well-preserved but obviously ancient.

Each road in town seemed to lead to the docks, emphasizing the past and present economic impact of fishing on the community. Casper could smell the salt in the air and the rotting fish before he turned the corner and saw the dock. The parking lot was one-third full, and most of the vehicles were small pick-up trucks. Stepping through the gateway, Casper saw the boathouse's front door was propped open. It resembled a large shed made of stone and wood, with a plaque by the address revealing the year the structure was established.

"Hello?" Casper called, stepping up to the front door but not entering. Inside, he could see an empty front desk. A large white mug of steaming coffee suggested someone was around. "Is anyone here?"

There was a backroom with a swinging door separating it from this front office, and the heavy swinging door opened in toward the office. A large furry beast rushed from around the door and toward Casper, the paws pounding against the creaking floorboards.

Throwing his arms in front of his body, Casper shut his eyes tight, expecting the creature to reach its fangs for his throat. There was heavy pressure against his chest. There was no pain, but instead a rough wet sensation against his raised wrist. Peeking one eye open, Casper saw the beat had jumped up, front paws propped up against the front of his sweater, and the long toothy, mouth gaped open. A wide pink tongue licked Casper's hands. Behind the beast, a fluffy tail wagged left to right.

"Tagh, git down!" A man shouted, coming out from the back room. He was holding a folder thick with documents, and a new, unwrinkled newspaper on the other hand.

The dog dropped to all fours and retreated to the desk, lying down in front of the office chair. The man laughed and placed the papers in his hands on the desktop.

"He greets every new visitor with kisses," the man said, waving a hand from Casper to come in. "What can I do you for?"

"I'm here to meet Isla Muir," Casper wiped his slobber-covered hands on the sides of his sweater, hoping it wouldn't stain. "She said to ask Logan for her location."

"I am Logan Wallace," the man said, reaching out a hand, which Casper gave a firm shake, "The dock master. When you step out through the front door, you'll see each dock has letters. She's all the way at the end of lane A."

"She's number one?" Casper grinned, looking out the large window to see the mass of strung-up boats.

"Her family has lived in this town since before it was founded," Logan licked his index finger and opened the folder, picking up the first page, "I believe she's here now. The boat's name is Eimear."

"Thank you," Casper nodded, glanced at the now-snoring dog, and left the boathouse.

Among the boats, there were only two or three fancy yachts. The rest were fishing boats for charter boats, built for heavy action and less so for luxury. At the end of lane A, a forty-five-foot boat bobbed against the floating dock. Classic rock blasted from somewhere on board, and Casper was surprised to hear the American music. He expected to hear Scottish banjo strings and fiddles like he experienced during his travel to the small town, and was relieved to hear the change in genre. Not that he listened to Pink Floyd and the Eagles regularly at home, but it reminded him of his father's summer barbeques. The overly-sugary lemonade his mom would make.

"Isla?" Casper stepped as close as possible to the side of the boat, not wanting to step on the deck without permission. "Isla Muir!"

His voice must have been heard over the blasting music because a tall, muscular woman ran up the stairs from the cabin below and looked straight at Casper.

"Hi!" She yelled over, walking over to the sheltered hull. The volume of the music lowered and the woman came back out. "I'm Isla. You're Casper Shaw?"

"I am," Casper reached his hand over the edge and shook her hand. Her grip was firm, her skin soft and warm against his.

"Come aboard!" She pulled away and stepped to the side, allowing Casper room to hop on.

Grabbing a rope, Casper climbed over the short railing and stepped onto the deck. The boat moved with the waves, and it took a few moments for him to get his footing.

"Sorry about the music," Isla said, gesturing to an oversized boombox on the floor next to the hull, "I like to listen when I'm cleaning."

"I don't mind," Casper grinned, running his hand through his hair. "There's so much room on board."

"I like to keep it minimalist," she said, waving her hands as if to present the shiny, neat exterior. Casper could almost see his reflection in the floorboards. "We can store your diving equipment here—" she pointed to the right of the boat, where a storage box rested open and empty, "-and let me show you the cabin."

Casper followed her down the steps, noticing the sun-bleached highlights in her light brown hair. Below decks, bright lamps lit every inch of space. The floors were swept and clear of clutter. The small kitchenette in one of the corners was bleach-white, the sparse silverware appearing unused, and the basic cream-colored linen on the four small beds laundered and tucked hospital-style.

"This is your bed," Isla pointed to the bed closest to the small bathroom, which also showed pristine conditions and a full container of lemon-scented foam hand soap, "And under the bed is a water-proof storage container—" she gently kicked a black box that hid under the cot, "will you be keeping your stuff at your rental?"

"I don't have much," Casper said, "So I'll store my belongings here for the trips."

"If you want," Isla offered, "You can keep your stuff here until all your trips are completed, instead of moving them from here to your rental and back."

"I'd prefer to keep all my stuff with me," he smiled, hoping his uneasy feeling didn't show through his bared teeth.

"That's quite alright," Isla shrugged, walking to the kitchenette, "The option is there if you change your mind. The fridge is fully stocked."

Opening the refrigerator door, Isla presented neat but crowded shelves. There were fresh apples and pears, chicken, bacon, butter, milk, condiments, etc. He wondered if, between the two of them, they would require such a large quantity of calories. But then he thought about his previous diving adventures and the ravenous attitude following. No morsel of food would go to waste nor rot.

"I'll cook each meal," Isla closed the door and opened a cabinet above the sink, showing a small collection of alcoholic beverages, "And these are for the evenings, as the sunsets on the Firth are seen nowhere else. I understand you're here for work, but there will be times to enjoy yourself."

Laughing, Casper shoved his hands in his pant pockets. "I've been on charter boats before, and this is very well put together. Thank you."

"I want each day away from solid land to feel special," Isla led him up to the main deck, "But also cost covers all the amenities."

"Right," Casper remembered this was a paid service and pulled out his wallet. "Here you go."

He handed her the roll of cash and watched her un-manicured fingers accept it and stuff it into her coat pocket. She smiled up at him and nodded.

"Do you know what dive shop you're renting from?" She asked, her hands resting on her hips.

"Billy Bobs?" Casper answered, raising an eyebrow. "When I was talking to them, back when I was planning the trip, they referred me to you for a charting service."

The smile on Isla's lips was replaced with an annoyed scowl, but after a moment, the woman was grinning again.

"Bill has some good deals," she nodded, turning to face the town, "He's a quirky man, though."

"Business is business," Casper felt awkward as if he just stepped into local drama. "But I'm heading there next. Thanks for the tour."

"See you tomorrow morning," Isla waved as Casper stepped back onto the dock.

As he walked up the dock, he could hear the stereo's volume rising, blasting Bonnie Tyler, and a faint hum along with the tune.

Chapter 3 - Kelsey

Kelsey Vargas felt the surge of energy from the crowd around him. The excitement of window shopping, the thrill of purchasing, and the enjoyment of selling and obtaining payment. It was an ecosystem thriving on objects, a game of speech, and barter, and he was an experienced player.

"This fabric was made for Charles III of Spain," Kelsey whispered to James, a skeptical tailor who owned a clothing shop on the bustling street of Tarbert, Harris, "But it was in competition for the silk brought from China, which he would eventually wear at his forty-seventh birthday celebration last winter."

"Why would I buy the second best?" The tailor asked, his accent thick of the Outer Hebrides. "Why buy the unwanted rags of royalty?"

"The foreign king may not have used this for a costume" Kesley ran his thumb over the dirt-free cloth, letting the threads shine in the sunlight glistening through the storefront windows, "But he did use it for the bedding of one of his mistresses."

Having dealt with young James before, Kelsey knew the man had an interest in strange fabrics with carnal myths. When James wasn't sewing the best frocks and suits for lairds and lords, the tailor was off participating in private acts often frowned upon and, in most places, illegal and punishable by death. All Kesley cared for was the price James was willing to pay.

"The cloth isn't even cut," James pulled the fabric over his fingers, the ends slipping out of Kelsey's hands.

"You can make it into anything you desire," Kelsey snapped his fingers, bringing James' attention back to the present. "After you purchase it."

There were a few moments of haggling, but only a few, before Kesley exited the front door with a hefty pouch of the coin in his inside coat pocket. The sun beat through the clouds, and the day was unusually warm and sticky. He fell into step with the flow of the crow, letting the energy carry him to the tavern on the corner of the town. Inside, he found his many crewmembers drowned in beer and covered in ladies.

Sitting down at the bench, Kelsey patted the shoulder of a small young boy.

"Keeping them in check, I see," Kelsey grinned as the boy looked up. When he saw his son's rich dark eyes and curls flop around his forehead, Kelsey had to take a moment to regain his breath and speech.

"I did my best, father," David said, picking at a plate of cubed potatoes with his fingers.

"Indeed, you have," Kelsey glanced across the table at Mateo, his first mate. "They all could afford? No debts?"

"None so far, sir," Mateo answered, raising a mug to his lips. "Now you're here, I can sink my face into that redhead's tits."

He gestured his mug to a busty woman at the bar, whose eyes hadn't left Mateo since Kelsey had sat down.

"You've earned it," Kelsey tossed a coin to the sailor, who caught it mid-air. "Enjoy your hard-earned pay."

Both father and son watched Mateo saunter over to the redhead, who smiled and led him up the stairs. David shook his head, a scowl on his face.

"Women are disgusting," he said, picking up a chicken leg and biting into the meat, "And everyone acts weird when they're around."

"In a few years," Kelsey ground Mateo's plate of leftovers and chewed on the potatoes, "You'll act weird around women, too. They won't be disgusting no longer."

"That's what Mateo says," David said. "He also says women find us disgusting, but whenever I see them, they are always joining us for dinner."

"You'll understand," Kesley chuckled, "In time."

The merchant was happy. His men were happy. Their activities were rambunctious but joyful, contained inside the walls of a tolerant tavern, familiar with sailors and soldiers and travelers. The scene was so serene that Kelsey felt the light air shift, grow heavier, when a figure entered through the front door and approached his table.

Turning toward the figure in a casual gesture, Kelsey saw the tall, broad-shouldered man wearing a cap that covered half his face, which was stern and focused. A white beard covered his lips, chin, and neck, but he was bald above the ears. The way he held himself, the way he walked, suggested he was one local Highlander brought up in times before the Jacobite Rebellion. As Kelsey looked up into the man's eyes, he wondered what the man lost before, during, and after Culloden.

"Are ya the one called Kesley Vargas?" the man asked in a deep voice.

"What did he say?" David asked, his ears not yet trained to heavy accents.

"Hush," Kelsey told the boy, then looked back up at Highlander, "I am."

"The Laird of the MacLeod Clan has invited you to his celebration tonight," the man held out a letter toward Kelsey, who took it with hesitant fingers. "He requests your presence."

The Highlander left. Kelsey opened the letter and read the invitation.

"Are you in trouble?" David asked, worry brimming his eyes.

Kelsey gave an abrupt laugh, shaking his head. "No, son. I'm going to see an old friend. You don't mind watching the boys again?"

The boy grinned, shrugging. "Only if I can drink the rest of your ale."

One eye squinting, Kelsey gave the boy a serious look. Then he slid the mug over to him and stood. "You know my rules."

"Mhmm," the boy picked the mug up with both hands and brought the rim to his lips.

Patting the boy's head, Kelsey felt the sack of recently-acquired coins and sighed. "Guess I'll have to see James, again."

Chapter 4 - Isla

Isla had felt the first encounter with Casper Shaw was pleasant, though she wouldn't have been so enthusiastic about accepting his trip request if she had known Bill was his referral. As much as she enjoyed the business, she hated when her former lover took part in it. Her business was her own, and her fathers, and Bill no longer had any say, wasn't allowed to give input in how the business was run.

Bill meant well, but he still cared for Isla even when she made it clear she no longer loved him. They dated all throughout secondary school, and a few years long-term when she was at university. He took over his father's dive shop and helped her father with the charter business, which Isla will always be thankful for. Since she moved back, Bill was always reaching out, offering assistance or discounts at his shop. She always refused. The less she had to see his sweet, scruffy beard, the better off she was.

That's why, once she finished cleaning the Eimear, she took the long way around town to get to the bank. Billy Bob's was located on Main Street and was the most direct route to the bank. But Isla didn't want to deal with him, so she drove two streets over, then took a left and parked in front of the bank. Still, she could see the old white and red flag looming down the road, flapping in the light breeze.

Stepping out of her truck, Isla wondered if Casper was there now. He probably was, trying on wetsuits and buoyancy devices. She thought about him zipping them up while onboard, the skin on his back bare for her to witness. As she stepped through the double doors of the bank, the thoughts of Casper's possible physique ran through her mind.

"Hi, Carla," she stepped up to the bank teller, "I'm depositing cash."

The short woman with a blonde bond worked on the deposit. Isla tapped her sneaker against the floor, waiting patiently, when she heard high heels tapping behind her.

"Oh, is that Isla Muir?" A high-pitched voice said, and Isla found it eerily familiar.

Looking behind her, Isla saw a skinny woman of medium height. She was wearing a bright pink blouse, a black pencil skirt, and matching pink heels. A black purse hung from her tiny elbow. Her smile was wide, her teeth straight and white.

"Yes, and who are..." Isla squinted at the woman, "Chloe?"

The woman rushed up to Isla and threw her arms around her white-and-blue flannel-clad shoulders. Isla placed her hand on Chloe's elbow, not ready to let her excitement show.

"Here's your receipt," Carla said, and Isla grinned in apology at the commotion and took the slip of paper.

"How have you been?" Isla asked her oldest friend, who used to wear blue jeans and low-cut tank tops.

"Fantastic," Chloe said, no longer bearing the thick country accent Isla still kept despite her university days. "I didn't know you were still in town."

"Yeah," Isla ran her hand through her messy hair, feeling a bit shabby standing next to the other woman. "I haven't dealt with everything yet."

"I'm *so* sorry to hear about your father," Chloe placed her hand on Isla's arm, drawing out the word 'so'. "I went to the funeral but haven't had a chance to come by the house. Are you planning on selling? I'm sure you are, all those memories. Unless you want to have something to remember him by."

Taking a step toward the door, Isla forced the corner of her lips up. "I haven't really thought about it, frankly."

"Alex can help you if you want to put it on the market," Chloe held her hand out to a man, who had been approaching her from one of the desks. "Have you met my husband, Alexander?"

"I haven't," Isla reached her hand out and shook the man's hand. She had noticed that he was new to the town since the last time she had visited, before her father's death, but a lot of new people have settled here. "Are you the new realtor?"

The lanky man was only a few inches taller than Chloe, whose drastic height was in fault of her heels. Alex had a humble face, no definition between his jaw and neck, and his eyes were kind, a dull grey that hid under unruly, thick eyebrows.

"Well, I wouldn't say new," he laughed, his tone businesslike, "I've been working here for about three years now."

Has it really been that long since I last visited Dad? Isla nodded, blinking, looking from Chloe to Alex.

"So you have a house to sell?" Alex asked after an awkward minute.

"Yes," Chloe said, hopping on the balls of her feet, the only part supporting her, "You remember that old brink detached one over on the southeast of town? The one with the vines on the side?"

"The one with the overgrown yard?" Alex lowered his voice as if the house was haunted.

"That's the one," Chloe giggled, flashing *forgive me* eyes at Isla, "Well, her Dad passed a few months ago, and—"

"I'm not selling it!" The word burst out of Isla's mouth in such a rush that she thought someone else had spoken, but when all the customers in the bank gave her surprised eyes, she blushed red. "I'm sorry, but I'm not ready to make that decision yet."

Before her old childhood friend or her rich husband could say anything else, Isla turned and hurried out the front doors. She jumped into her truck, backed out of the parking spot, and drove as fast as the speed limit allowed past Billy Bob's Dive Shop.

Back at the house, Isla turned the truck off in the gravel driveway and stared out at the yard. The white picket fence had once been a cute addition to the property but now appeared to be a prison for the twisting green weeds that reached past the dull pointed arrow reaching for the clouds. The once-romantic vibrant vines on the north face of the house now conquered the brick, growing along the roof and thick bushes. The house looked deserted, abandoned, even though someone has always lived here for the last thirty years or so.

The inside could raise the opposite conclusion, suggesting someone never left the house in thirty years. *What was Dad thinking?* Thinking about the passage of time, Isla remembered she had visited. It was right after she started her own research on the east coast. The grass had been mowed, and there was even a garden in front of the street view windows with vegetables and flowers. She remembered finding her father tending the garden every morning before making her breakfast.

Sighing, Isla climbed out of her truck and walked up to the front door. Inside, she put her purse on the small free spot on the dining table. She thought about what she would need on the boat for the three-day trip, and remembered she already had extra clothes and toiletries stores on board. She really didn't have to come back to the house every night, and she could live on the boat if she wanted to. Checking on the house, though, felt like a responsibility, even if she was letting it go to ruin.

Pouring herself another bowl of cereal, Isla followed her evening routine and went up to her bedroom. This was the only room not in disarray, except for the dirty dish from last night. Curling up in her bed, she ate cereal for dinner and read a trashy romance novel from her mother's old collection. Her father had kept all of his late wife's possession, storing them in a spare closet in the upstairs hallway. When Isla had attempted organizing the house, she had opened the closet and found only one stack of books. Instead of nonfiction, though, these books were all fictional, dramatized, with sweaty, muscle men and desirable women on the front covers.

Isla had laughed at her mother's choice of reading but now found herself getting lost in the fantasy. Written sex distracted Isla, and she needed anything to procrastinate.

Chapter 5 - Casper

Casper had no trouble finding the dive shop in the middle of town. He simply followed Main Street from his rental until he saw the diving flag, and the gaudy wooden sign: BILLY BOB'S DIVE SHOP. The only other shop that was as flashy as this one was the global coffee chain on the corner, one block away. Even the smallest of destinations will provide commercial caffeine needs to travelers.

The dive shop appeared small on the outside, with a narrow door and small window displaying the newest shipment of wetsuits, regulators, and oxygen tanks. Once Casper entered through the door, though, he saw that the building was much larger on the inside. The rows of available equipment seemed to never end.

"'Ello?" A voice called from behind a rack of wetsuits near the counter.

"Hey," Casper called back, his eyes scanning for a face. "I'm Casper Shaw. I'm here to pick up the rentals I ordered."

"Och, nice to finally meet ye," the man filled out his knit sweater well, with a beard that seemed to stick out in every direction except neat. "I'm Bill. Ye're stuff is right over here."

Bill showed him to an organized pile of necessary equipment. There were enough oxygen tanks for each dive for all three days, and backup regulators, buoyancy compensators, computer, and extra weights.

"You need help loading your car?" Bill asked, looking ready to pick up one of the tanks.

"Uh," Casper scratched the back of his head, "I thought you said you delivered equipment to the dock."

The dive shop owner raised an eyebrow, his grin fading. "You didn't pay for the service online."

"I didn't know you charged that," Casper felt jilted, crossing his arms over his chest, "I didn't rent a car."

"You come to the country without a vehicle?" Bill laughed, the noise carrying throughout the store. "You expect everyone to just drop their shifts and help you out?"

"I'm sorry," Casper felt panic set into his blood, "Can I pay you to bring it over today?"

Mumbling incoherently, Bill stepped behind the desk and looked at a calendar tacked to the wall. He ran his finger along a written list and then threw his hand up in the air.

"Where do you need me to drop it off?"

"Isla Muir's boat?"

The dive shop owner's ears perked, and he turned quickly to face Casper.

"Why didn't you say so before?" He exclaimed, laughing. "You actually hired her?"

"You told me she was the best," Casper was smiling but he didn't feel happy. The situation was weird and he wanted to go back to his room as soon as possible.

"She is," Bill nodded, grabbing a set of keys, "She is. Come on, then."

"Huh?" Casper watched the man go to the front door and prop it open.

"Let's load my truck and drop it off!" Bill came back and picked up two oxygen tanks, showing his strength as he carried each one under his arms. "No charge."

It took about ten minutes to load the truck waiting outside by the curb. The short drive to the dock was silent as Bill hummed to a radio tune in Gaelic. Casper stared out at the town passing by, feeling out of place. As the sun lowered in the sky, above the water, casting moving orange glowing slices as the waves rolled toward the sand and cliffs, Casper and Bill used a rolling cart to bring the equipment to the boathouse. Logan was still sitting at his desk, reading the same newspaper, which was now creased and stained with coffee rings.

"Isla isn't here," Logan said as the two men came in through the door, "But you can leave the cart of equipment in the corner over there. I lock up every night."

"Is that alright?" Bill asked, pushing the cart through the open doorway.

"Of course, Billy Boy!" Logan flipped the page of the newspaper. Tagh approached Bill and licked his hand, his tail wagging at a leisure pace. "You know you're welcome here, but you need to give the girl some space."

"Logan, come on."

"No, no," Logan chugged the last of his coffee and walked to the swinging doors of the back room, "You should find a girl who wants the same things as you."

"Isla does, though," Bill followed the older man into the backroom, but their voices still carried into the front office. Casper shifted from one foot to the other, eyeing the dog who laid back down under the desk.

"You know and I know," Logan's voice could be heard faintly, "That she will move on from here, again, once she has handled the house and the business. She isn't meant to stay in one place for long, and you'll die in this town."

"If she's going to leave," Bill said, his voice also muffled by the door, "She would've done it. She had a whole life over there, and she dropped everything to come here."

"It wasn't for you, Bill," Logan's tone turned snarky, "But because her father died. Reason enough to 'drop everything' and need a moment to rethink her life. She has no family, no prospects except the boat and house that everyone is itching for her to sell. The best thing for us is to support her."

"I'm trying to support her!" Bill's voice raised, sounding desperate.

"The only way for you to help Isla is if you let her go."

Both men returned to the front office, Logan with a fresh cup of hot coffee, Bill with a distressed frown. They looked at Casper as if they had forgotten he was there.

"Sorry 'bout that," Bill cleared his throat, "Where you staying tonight? Need a ride?"

"No, thank you," Casper gave a polite grin, stepping backward toward the front door, "I appreciate your help and all. I'll see you in a few days with the rentals."

"Glad to do business with you," Bill waved a hand before crouching down to give Tagh affection, who lifted his head and panted.

Outside, the air felt lighter and Casper sucked in lungfuls. Even after a day in the town, the drama felt too much. Casper had thought these tiny seaside villages were quiet, holding people with perfect lives. *I guess every place has its stories.*

Chapter 6 - Kelsey

James did not hold back from dressing Kelsey in the finest linens. The outfit was appropriate for a Laird's banquet, but tiny details suggested Kesley wasn't normal townsfolk from the Highlands. Contrasting with the dark blue vest, the sleeve hems had delicate stitching of orange, which matched the laces of the heeled shoes. The trousers were a matching blue, and tucked into the waistline was a crisp white blouse.

Kelsey at first slapped James' hand away when the tailor reached for the merchant's long dark curls. But after being reminded of the local hairstyles of men, he let his hair get brushed and pulled into a plait running down the back of his head. He liked to feel his hair loose around his neck and face and felt constricted with it tied back.

"A proper gentleman," James gave Kelsey a small mirror.

"Aren't I usually." He barely looked at himself before handing the mirror back.

"Of course, sir."

Kelsey left the shop and noticed heads turning. While people normally noticed him, they looked at him with a mix of wonder and fear. Now, they all had respect and interest in their eyes, and a few ladies grinned in his direction before hiding behind scarves. The last time he felt like this was during a party in Paris, where he would only expect to see this kind of costume. Uncomfortable fashion. Impractical. Itchy. He hated heels.

After finding a carriage for transport, Kelsey climbed into the seat and sat on the worn cushion seat. The wheels bumped along the rocks and mud that infested the road leading to the castle, which rose up on a hill overlooking the town. The sun was going down, and candles lit every window of the building. In the front entrance gates, guests entered mainly by foot. There were a few other carriages, others arrived by horseback. The garments worn by everyone were reused from previous gatherings, the kinds of clothes a household only took out of storage once or twice a year.

"Shall I wait, sir?" The driver asked as Kelsey climbed out of the passenger's box.

"Don't believe that'll be necessary," he told the man, who looked surprised. "I'll find my way back to town."

"It's a long way, sir," the driver spoke up, looking over Kelsey's buffed shoes and laundered stockings, "And you'll ruin your costume."

"I appreciate your concern," Kelsey smiled, and the man seemed to relax from the gesture, "But I'll do without your service. Here."

He handed an extra stack of coins to the driver, whose eyes widened from the generous tip.

"Thank you, sir," the driver nodded, pocketing the coins carefully into his pocket.

As the driver rode off, Kelsey turned and entered through the gate. None of the guards stopped to question him, even though he was on the edge of appearing a cheap businessman. While he thrived on hard, good bargains, he ensured those around him felt appreciated and satisfied with the haggling.

Following the crowd, Kelsey walked into the castle's hallways and tried not to look surprised. Much has changed since he last had visited. There was more light, more laughter. He remembered how dark the stone walkways were, and the depressing atmosphere that made every servant and resident feel worse about their miserable lives. This time around, even the servants holding platters of food seemed to be happily eager to stuff the visitor's guests with appetizers and wine.

Inside the great hall, numerous tables were positioned in rows and angles, the purpose being for everyone to have the chance to interact with neighboring tables and to be able to see the singular long table at the front of the room. Here, the Laird would sit with his family and closest companions. There was even a spot for the hounds to chew on scars at the end of each table.

Kelsey had small talk with a few groups, talking about the unchanging gloomy weather or about the wondrous decorations of the hall.

"I can't believe they would pay for purple banners," said Lord Murphy, who lived outside of the town. "They must have paid all our taxes just for the few."

"Or he simply used the taxes meant for the King," said a merchant, whose three teenage daughters stood behind him. They all stared at Kelsey while trying not to look obviously interested. While they all had rosy cheeks and ample bosoms, Kelsey wasn't interested and barely glanced at their round faces.

"And the number of candles!" The Lord exclaimed, holding a glass of wine close to his double chin. "We don't need to see every crevice in his home, do we? We only had one candle to share last winter, and my wife used it for her mundane reading."

"Her father shouldn't have sent her to lessons," the merchant mumbled, gesturing his elbow to his daughters, "Women are meant for the housework while we slave at desks."

While two of the daughters nodded in agreement, the smaller girl lowered her eyes to her feet. Kelsey saw the disappointment in her face, and he wanted to tell her to hold onto hope. But he didn't want to interfere and start a war.

"Would you let your wife read, sir?" The lord asked, looking at Kelsey.

"Yes," he said, trying not to look smug when the group shared surprised faces, "Though my wife passed many years ago. She enjoyed poetry, though I could never find a poem that interested me. Still, I kept quiet and let her read to me sonnets and villanovas every night. She had a lovely voice."

"Widowed, you say?" The merchant pressed his three daughters in front of him. "What is your line of employment?"

Sighing, Kelsey took a sip of wine. "I am a captain of a merchant ship. I can never take a wife after the first, for no one could replace her."

"A man needs a wife, though," the merchant used the same convincing tone that Kelsey used when selling his goods, "Not for love, but to do chores and even for companionship, children."

Looking at each of the three young women, Kelsey's eyes landed on the smaller one. She appeared to be seventeen, but her sad face made her look older and wiser. Holding his hand out, Kelsey smiled at the girl.

"I'm not looking for a wife," he said, "But I am looking for a dance partner. May I?"

The girl searched her father's face for permission, and with it, she took Kelsey's hand. He led her to the dance floor, where a bunch of brave couples was stepping and jumping to the three-instrument band.

"Do you know how to dance?" Kelsey asked.

"No," the girl looked terrified and excited at the same time, her cheeks flushing.

"Good," he said, whispering in her ear, "I don't either."

They began twirling and skipping to the tune of the fiddle as the drum was off-beat, and they mimicked what the other couples were doing. Kelsey kicked his knees up high, and the girl spun under his arm. She gave a small laugh, breathing hard just as he was. While running a ship was tough physical labor, dancing was a whole other activity. As the song ended, and before the new one began, Kelsey tried catching his breath and pulled the girl to the side.

"Thank you," he told her, clasping his hands behind his back, "I haven't had that much fun in a long time."

"Since your wife passed?"

Shocked, Kelsey stared down at the girl, who looked at her feet in embarrassment. He let out a laugh and nodded.

"You should know," he told her, "I will not court you, nor any woman in the world."

A tear escaped down the girl's cheek as she nodded.

"You shouldn't expect a marriage to save you," Kelsey glanced across the room at her father, who was presenting his other two daughters to another male suitor. "I can tell you expect more than wifely duties, and you shouldn't give up on those dreams you have."

"My father won't let me go," she spoke quietly, "Not without a man's hand in marriage."

"I know," Kelsey didn't understand why he was wasting his time with this girl, but he felt it was his responsibility to encourage those with adventurous souls. "But don't lose faith that things will turn in your favor. What's your name?"

"Beth."

"Well, Beth," Kelsey bowed to her, grinning, "Pleasure meeting you. I have some business to attend to, but I pray your evening goes well."

Saying nothing, Beth curtsied and took little steps to join her father. Just then, the Highlander from the tavern approached Kelsey.

"The Laird will meet with you after the feast," the Highlander informed him.

"Where is he now?" Kelsey noticed the Laird's designated area was still empty.

That's when the music died down and every visitor hushed, standing to face the great hall doors. In walked Laird Thomas MacLeod, with his thick red hair pulled back in a leather tie. His eyes scanned the crowd, and when they landed on Kelsey's face, the shadow of a smile spread on the Laird's lips.

Hello, old friend.

Chapter 7 - Isla

Isla could barely sleep, tossing and turning in her bed, thinking about being away from the house for two nights. The house would be fine. *She* would be fine. As much as she hated coming back to the house and seeing the mess, she hated leaving. The situation was unhealthy, she knew, but nothing propelled her into action. She had no energy to start in a room and clean.

Forty-five minutes before her alarm went off, the faint grey light outside her window woke her up from her half-conscious slumber. Sitting up, she rubbed crusties out of her eyes and yawned. She watched the light grow against the curtains on her window until her alarm did go off, and she crawled out of bed. She pulled on a pair of clean pants and a sweater and grabbed all the dirty dishes on the nightstand.

The only tidying she did in the house was from her own uncleanliness. The long hair in the bathtub, the dirty clothes in the hamper, and the trash that needed to be taken out for tomorrow's pickup. She kept imaginary blinders up, like the ones used to keep labor horses focused, so she wouldn't see the other things she needed to clean. One day, she would. But not now.

Grabbing two romance novels, Isla locked up the house and hopped into her truck. As she drove down the road to the docks, she glanced once in her rearview mirror as the house disappeared from sight. The muscles in her neck hurt, either from the uncomfortable sleeping positions or from anxiety.

No matter how early Isla arrived at the boathouse, Logan was already there, alert as much as the old man could be. All he did every day, besides drink coffee and read the newspaper, was keep track of the liberated boating schedule, bills, and fees for dock use, and maintaining the docks and parking lot. If he wasn't sitting at the office desk, he was scrubbing the piers or trimming bushes on the edge of the property. Tagh would always be near him, laying on the ground panting and snoring. While his purpose was to ward off visitors with ill-intentions, the dog did nothing else but lounge.

"Your diver dropped off his stuff last night," Logan pointed at a grouping of diving equipment in the corner of the room, "With Bill."

Groaning, Isla knelt down and ran her fingers through Tagh's heavy mane. The dog almost purred, pressing his neck against her hand.

"At least I didn't have to pick up the supplies," Isla said, sniffing the aroma of coffee beans, "Can I grab a mug?"

"You know where it is."

Isla went through the swinging door and poured herself a cup of coffee. It wasn't as hot, but it was still delicious as she drank half of the liquid in one gulp. Coming back out to the front office, she sat on a beat-up green couch across from the desk, tucking her feet underneath her.

"You need to talk?" Logan set his newspaper down and looked directly at her, which he rarely did.

"No," she shook her bread, taking small sips of her coffee to fill her time.

"You look like you've been thinking."

"I'm always thinking," she told him, looking into the brown abyss of caffeine, "I just feel stuck."

Instead of saying anything, Logan leaned back in his chair and laced his fingers together, resting them on his belly.

"I just don't..." Isla could feel the confusing emotions and anger rising up, filling the back of her throat, but she chugged the rest of her coffee and shook her head. "I'm fine. I'll see you in a few days, Logan."

She could feel the man's eyes on her back as she went to the backroom to rinse her cup. As she walked back through to the front door, he had picked his newspaper back up.

"Don't be too hard on yourself," he said before she reached the doorframe. "But also don't be afraid to let people listen."

She tapped the door frame with two knuckles, looking back at him.

"Thanks," she murmured before walking down to her boat.

The day before, Isla had already done any necessary preparations for the trip. Still, she checked her boat over, looking for signs of wear and tear, and any hint of faulty gears. Then she sat on her bunk, the one farthest from Casper's designated area, and continued reading the novel she had fallen asleep with last night.

After an hour, the sound of wheels on the dock echoed down the open hatch for the stairs. Bookmarking her page, Isla went up to greet her customer.

"Good morning," she called, waving one hand as she held the other to shield her eyes from the sun.

"Hello," Casper stopped the cart of equipment next to the boat and faced her, hands on his hips, "Should we start?"

It took about thirty minutes for the supplies to be loaded, strapped and secured, and to be triple-checked for faults or cracks. Satisfied with the safety of her customer, Isla stepped back and grinned.

"I hope you had a good night's rest," she told Casper, who looked more tired than she felt.

There were dark bags under his eyes, and the clean-shaven chiseled jaw had light stubble. When the sun touched his face, some of the tiny hairs looked golden, matching some of the highlights that mixed with the darker blonde waves. He reminded her of what a classic American man looked like, and she imagined him surfing in hot California, only wearing bright-colored swim trunks with large flowers printed on the fabric. His sophisticated attitude and button-up shirt, and the fact that he didn't say "Dude", reminded Isla that he wasn't a stereotype.

"I stayed up late reading," Casper said, rubbing his hand over his chin. "Woke up late."

"You got here on time," Isla looked out at the tide, "Perfect timing, actually. If there's nothing else you need, we can head out."

"Take me to sea," he smiled, handing her a piece of paper. "These are the coordinates for each day. I know I gave them to you through email, but I just wanted to make sure they were right."

Taking the paper, Isla read the list of numbers. Today, she would be driving him out to the north section of the firth. The next few days would be spent at two different locations in those regions, where he would search for a specific species of nudibranch.

"It'll take a few hours to get out there," she said, glancing at the flag on her boat and the height of the waves, "You can rest up and I'll let you know when we're close."

"No, I'll stay up," he said, walking toward the stairs, "Do some more reading."

"Alrighty," she went to the hull and started the engine. She heard the soft thuds of his footsteps as he descended the stairs, and then all she could hear was the rumbling of the Eimear.

Just like driving a car, Isla's eyes and mind went on autopilot. She knew where the coordinates were, so she stared out at the horizon, occasionally checking the compass, speed, and radio as she navigated toward the far north. She let her brain dwindle back to the book she was reading. She could see the characters acting out the latest scene she read.

The heroine had refused the hero's hand in marriage, even though she was in love with him. She refused because the hero was rumored to be involved in a scandalous partnership with some other woman, but only the reader knows that the rumor isn't true. As ridiculous as the situation was, Isla found herself intrigued and entertained by the chapter. Now, as she let the scene play out in her mind like a movie, she imagined Casper as the hero. It was simply where her mind went, and she let her thoughts run wild to pass the time.

Chapter 8 - Casper

The rocking of the boat and the soft pillow guided Casper into a deep sleep, despite his attempt to stay away. He had tried sitting at the small table near the kitchenette, but then he felt a little nauseous so laid down. Holding his notebook above him wore his arms out, so he rested it facedown on his chest, closed his eyes...

When he opened them up, the world seemed different in the way it does after taking an unexpected nap. The light coming down from the stairs was brighter, suggesting the position of the sun was at its highest.

Checking his watch, Casper saw an hour and a half had gone by. He grabbed the notebook on his chest and placed it under his pillow, hidden from wandering eyes. Not that he didn't trust Isla, but he knew how curious people could be.

Heading up to the main deck, he saw the woman standing in the hull, scanning the sea in front of the boat. Casper leaned against the stair railing and watched her, taking her appearance in before he made his presence known. He wasn't trying to be creepy, but he found it difficult to look at her when talking to her. When he tried meeting her eye when she spoke, a powerful magnet pushed against his gaze. So he would look at his feet, her shoulder, behind her, anywhere but her intelligent eyes. The way she looked at him felt like she was analyzing his brain, which made him worry that she could read through his lies.

As she faced away from him, Casper looked her up and down. Her brown hair was pulled in a low ponytail, messy but curly. She wore an oversized sweater that hid the tiny waist he had witnessed yesterday, but the blue jeans she wore fit against the curves of her bottom and legs. Dirty wellies hid her feet and ankles, and she was tapping to a song blasting on the boombox. When Casper had scheduled the charter service, he had expected Isla's father to run the trips. From what he's gathered, though, the old man wasn't around anymore.

A seagull came down and landed on the deck, startling Casper. He ascended the rest of the steps and waved at the bird, hoping it would fly away. It took a step back, its black marble eyes not blinking as it stared at the man.

"Be nice to Jessie," Isla called over, making Casper turn to see her watching the confrontation, "He's a guest on this boat and gives me good luck."

"How can you tell him apart?" Casper went to the hull so he could hear her better, and be further away from the bird.

"See the black spot on his wind?" Isla pointed at the bird, and sure enough, there was a black coloration in the shape of the letter *J*, "No other gull has that. They all have their white and grey colors, but not any marks like that.

"How do you know he isn't some species of gull?" Casper asked, playing the educated route. He grinned, expecting her to say something in awe and wonder.

"Because I research it," Isla said, laughing, "Or, at latest one of my friends back at work did. He works on coastal birds."

"Your work?" Casper raised an eyebrow, a nasty weight sinking from his chest to his belly. "I thought this was your work."

"At the moment, this is," Isla explained, her tone carefree, "But I'm a researcher over on the east coast. I've taken some time off."

Casper's throat felt dry. "A researcher of what?"

"Marine biology," the words came out sing-songy, probably finding it funny that Casper Shaw was one, too. "I study how parasitic infection affects the osmoregulation in salmon, and..."

Casper now stared directly at her face but could see it as her words faded from his thoughts. He was in so much trouble. He was going to be found out because he didn't do *his* research before booking this trip. She's going to figure out his real intentions, and kick him off or tell the police. Not that what he was doing was illegal, per say, but still frown upon. The most he was worried about was drawing the attention of other explorers. He didn't want the competition.

"But I know very little about invertebrates," Isla wrapped up her monologue, paused, and frowned at Casper, "Are you alright? Sorry if I rambled, I really get excited talking to other ecologists."

"Yes, I'm just surprised," Casper said, trying to regain his confidence, "How lucky I am to unknowingly work with someone in my field?"

"I told you Jessie was a good-luck charm," she looked forward and slowed the boat down, "You might want to suit up. We're almost at the first destination."

It took Casper a few minutes to change into fleece undergarments before sliding the thick drysuit over his limbs. His hands poked through the arm gaskets, and then he pulled his head through the head gasket and settled it around his neck. Zipping it up proved difficult as he couldn't reach where it started on his right shoulder.

"Got it?" Isla asked, standing nearby for assistance.

"Nope," Casper dropped his hands to his side in defeat.

"I'll get it," she came up to his side and pulled the zipper closed, tugging it across his chest, then folding the rubber seal over the opening. This was the closest she had been to him since they met, and Casper was trying not to notice.

With the zipper snug, Casper pulled his wet boots on and crouched down to push the air out of the drysuit as much as possible. The suit felt vacuum-sealed, which meant he did it right. It had been a few months since he last dived.

He attached the first oxygen tank to the buoyancy compensator, hooked the octo regulator up to the tank, attached the dive computer to his wrist, and wrapped his weight belt around his waist. Checking his list, Casper made sure every little important item was attached and ready to be used.

"Ready," he told the captain, who leaned against the railing on the port side of the boat.

"Show me your hand signals," she said, and he went through a series of hand movements.

All the other hand signals he knew were meant for a dive buddy, which most business required. Casper knew it was safer to have a partner going underwater with you, but he couldn't risk someone knowing about the treasure and getting hurt. That was another reason why Casper chose Isla: she was the first charter service that didn't ask about a diving buddy.

Isla ran her hands over the equipment, but it felt as if she were touching his skin. The sun beat down on the black material of his suit, and the heat was rising against his skin.

"All set," she told him, and he sat down.

One hand on his regulator and the other on his goggles, and he let himself fall backward into the water. The cold liquid rushed around him, and the air in his buoyancy compensator shot him to the surface. The water was cold against his lips and cheeks, but the rest of his body stayed warm. He expected it to be soothing from his previous state of warmth, but the shock almost caused him to spit out his regulator.

Bobbing on the surface, Casper looked up and saw Isla waiting for him to let him know he was safe. He tapped the top of his cap-covered head with one hand, signaling to the captain that he was okay. Then he slowly let the air out of his buoyancy compensator, a little at a time, and the surface of the waves rose above his head. The world darkened. Casper found himself floating deeper, eventually turning his flashlight on in search of gold.

Chapter 9 - Kelsey

Kelsey watched the crowd move to the tune of Laird Thomas MacLeod. The energy could be cut through with the sword on Kelsey's belt, but he felt relaxed. He didn't feel a threat or need to keep his hands prepared, though he was always ready for the unexpected. As any good traveler should act.

When Laird Thomas sat, his blood relatives followed suit, and a wave spread throughout the Great Manor as all guests settled into their benches at the long tables. No one picked up food until the Laird began eating, even if appetizers were previously bitten into. With a flick of the wrist from the Laird, the music started playing again, and chatter rose from every table.

Staying silent, Kelsey took a few small sips of wine, picking at the robust grape vine resting in front of him. His stomach demanded he fill his plate with every morsel of sustenance laid out before him, but he wanted to be quick on his toes. Eating too much slows his wit, and he needed a clear mind. Not that he was concerned, but whatever discussion was prepared with the Laird, he needed to be alert.

Next to the Laird was a round woman with fair hair, almost the color of the wax candles dripping on every candelabra placed throughout the room. From where Kelsey sat, it looked as if the woman didn't have any eyebrows. She didn't appear Scottish and wondered if Thomas decided to marry someone from abroad.

Sorry, *Laird* Thomas.

Kelsey wondered what would happen if he disrespected the Laird. Would the redhead laugh it off, or has the old boy let power change his youthful disposition for humility? No matter how many men Kelsey led, he was able to simultaneously demand respect from them but also support them as if they were brothers. It was a balance that many leaders didn't learn. Definitely wasn't an attribute Kelsey nor Thomas were born with, but the difference between nobility and the working class was that one didn't have to learn good leadership skills.

The feast ended, the candles insignificantly shorter but definitely changed. The Laird stood and began speaking in English, which surprised Kelsey. He knew the British would punish Thomas for showing any sign of the Scottish culture, but he was still disappointed.

"If everyone could stand with me," the Laird projected his voice, and the guests obeyed. "We join tonight to..."

There was a tap on Kelsey's shoulder, and he turned around to see the large Highlander who had invited him here. The Laird hadn't stopped talking, and everyone else was still listening. The large man signaled for Kelsey to follow him, and Kelsey stepped politely around the standing guests.

Stopping at a narrow side hallway, the man faced Kelsey and spoke in a whisper. "The Laird would like for you to wait for him in his study."

"How do I know you aren't ambushing me?" Kelsey was blunt, and not many people were used to such forwardness.

The man looked as if Kelsey had assaulted him. "The discussion is of the utmost importance. No one most know he spoke to you, or see you leave with him."

"Perhaps I shouldn't have arrived in such grandiose attire, then," Kelsey slid his thumb and finger along the delicate lining of his coat.

"Perhaps not," the man turned and began walking down the hallway, away from the dining hall.

Following, Kelsey placed his hand on the handle of his sword, keeping a light foot and some space between the man in front of him. He indeed was led up a series of stairs and hallways, ones he remembered from the last time he visited. The pathway was familiar, and his hand eased on his sword the further they walked.

They reached a wooden door, which had one armored guard standing post outside of it. The Highlander nodded at the guard, who nodded back and stepped to the side. The Highlander pushed the door open, presenting a well-furnished study. The upholstery of the furniture appeared old but maintained, and the desk was cluttered with papers, quills, and ink jars. A vast portrait hung from the wall behind the desk, and it showed Thomas, the blonde woman sitting next to Thomas during the feast, and a tiny boy with blonde hair the same as the woman. Kelsey remembered seeing the little one at the front table, his small head poking above the table. The painter was able to replicate the nose, which was a copy of Thomas'.

The door closed behind Kelsey, and he turned to see the Laird watching him carefully. The man, who Kelsey assumed was the Laird's manservant and bodyguard, stood by the door, arms crossed and staring into space.

"I wondered what you'd wear," Thomas stepped closer, one hand behind his back and the other up in the air, a finger pointing as if he was thinking. "I shouldn't be surprised but I am."

"Only the best linens for you, my *Laird*," Kelsey bowed, over-dramatic, testing his old friend.

Thomas raised one eyebrow and began to laugh. He clapped his hands together and grabbed Kelsey into a fierce hug. Something cracked in the merchant's back, and when he squeezed Thomas, it sounded like a rib broke. Neither man cared, grinning ear to ear.

Letting go, Thomas went to the desk and sat in his chair. "Please, sit."

Kelsey took the back of a chair and set it on the other side of the desk. Looking over the top of the surface, he met Thomas' eyes. "How does responsibility feel?"

"It's not as difficult as my father made it sound," Thomas said, organizing papers into multiple piles and cleaning up an ink spill, "The position has its moments where I feel... overwhelmed."

"What about the British?" Kelsey asked, leaning forward to lower his voice. "It seemed you've been keeping them happy."

Trepidation flicked across Thomas' face, and he sat back in his chair. "I have. For the most part. Our crops have been good, and our livestock. The businesses in town prove to be useful. Everyone has paid their rents."

"The price of giving up who you are, huh?" Kelsey's voice had a hint of steel in it, and he knew he was being harsh, but couldn't help the edge of disappointment.

"Not everyone can sail away from their enemies, Vargas," Thomas's own words became hard, and he almost sounded emotionally wounded. "I have a whole town full of families to take care of, while you have a little crew."

Running a hand over his face, Kelsey felt how tight the muscles around his eyes and mouth were. "Does your son understand the language of his people?"

"I've taught him what he needs to survive," Thomas gripped the arm of his chair, his knuckles turning white. "What have you done?"

Sudden embarrassment shot through Kelsey and he looked down at his hands. "I *do* understand, Thomas."

When Thomas didn't respond, Kelsey looked up to expect an offended expression. Instead, the Laird's face held empathy and sadness.

"How old, Kelsey?"

"Nine."

"Robert is five," Thomas grinned for a second, then leaned forward, "We do what we think will protect them in this new world, right?"

With a nod, Kelsey met his friend's eyes. "What do you need me to do?"

Thomas looked confused, with a spark of mischief in his eyes.

"I'm glad to have seen you, old friend," Kelsey shrugged, gesturing between himself and Thomas, "Yet I feel you wanted to meet for more urgent business."

"Well," Thomas glanced at the bodyguard before looking back at Kelsey, "I need you to do your job. I need you to smuggle something for me."

Chapter 10 - Isla

While Casper descended under the cold surface, Isla sits on a bench. In her lap is a bag of cheese crackers and one of the romance novels. With some attention on the water in case of early surfacing, she is sixty pages into the paperback. Her willpower to look away is low, and she shoves crackers into her mouth.

Many people say it isn't healthy to eat while distracted, but she finds it comforting. She also is always hungry as she is constantly working. She also doesn't care what people say as people say a lot of things that don't matter.

Finishing the last line of the page, Isla uses a sticky orange-coated finger to flip the thin paper. Her eyes devour words, voracious for the fantasy world. Sure, she lived in one of the most beautiful destinations on earth, but beauty was subjective, and she was used to the scenery. She still felt a grain of awe at the green jagged cliffs north of the coast, and the rolling hills further inland with their perfect stone walls. The clean, paved roads made her look twice, as well as the wildflowers on either side of the pavement. But then she would keep on driving, and think about her to-do list, or not-to-do list which was growing each day.

The annoying part of growing up in this town was that everyone knew her, everyone loved her, and most people would help her if she asked. The simplicity of it repulsed Isla, so she didn't bring it up. She knew Bill would close his shop for a week just to assist in cleaning out her father's house, but the last thing she wanted was to owe her ex-boyfriend, much less see him. Over the last two months, multiple townsfolk and neighbors reached out to Isla and offered their assistance. But she didn't want it.

She didn't want everyone to see how mad her father had become.

A loud squawk from Isla's feet made her jump, and she almost dropped the book over the side of the boat. Then she would've never known if the heroine gave in to the hero's sexy suggestion of meeting in the parlor, and Isla needed to know.

Jessie was watching her, or rather, the orange cardboard snack box in her lap.

"No!" She exclaimed, placing her hand over the opening flaps of the box, more possessively than she meant.

The bird turned its beak to the ground, almost in a dejected manner. Isla felt a sting of embarrassment and pity, and she sighed loudly.

"Fine," she opened the box and pulled a handful of crackers, "But if this gets out, I'm letting you starve."

She knew it was bad to feed wildlife, and even worse since she was a strong supporter of environmental responsibility and justice. But like her normal routine before the death of her father, she let impulse guide her. She placed the crackers on the end of the bench, sat back, and opened the book.

The bird didn't hesitate to peck at the crackers, grabbing one and throwing its head back, letting the food fall down its esophagus. The noises Jessie made were enough to make Isla laugh, and she watched until the bird was satisfied and flew away.

Many sailors say that seabirds were the souls of those lost at sea. Isla was a woman of science and facts, see it or *don't* believe it. Proof. Though growing up in a fishing town, she couldn't help to hold onto those tiny childhood fairytales. She knew Jessie came from a large mottled-colored egg from one of the cliffs up north, born from the multiplication of genes after the combination of sperm and egg. Just like the rest of multicellular animals. Though sometimes Isla wondered if Jessie was her father coming back to haunt her.

Technically, her father wasn't lost at sea. His body was found two days after he sailed away from the dock. Cause of death was drowning, boat and body found together in the water down south near a shallow inlet. No one knew why he had traveled there, or how he fell overboard.

Gossip said heart attack, but Isla knew from reports that it was simple as getting too much water in the lungs.

When Isla first learned of her father's death, she had wanted to know why, why, why. As the law enforcement officer explained to her the possible explanations, though, she tuned him out and realized she didn't care. Knowing how he died or how it *possibly* happened wasn't going to bring him back. And of all the fairytales Isla held on to, resurrection wasn't one of them. Just like the fictional novel in her hand, incarnation was a fantasy she liked to dwell on, distracting her from reality.

Curling her fingers into the box of crackers, Isla reached the crinkly bottom of the bag. She was still hungry, but didn't want to leave her post. Her wristwatch told her Casper would still be diving for another twenty minutes, but a little voice in her head told her she would only be gone for twenty seconds. Honestly, what could happen in such a short amount of time?

Glancing out at the waves, not calm but not showing signs of life except the little diving buoy on the surface, Isla stood and clutched the book and box. Turning, she rushed without running across the deck and down the stairs. She tossed the empty box into the open trash can near the table, opened the shelf by the fridge, grabbed another snack, and hurried back up the stairs. Her heart beat fast, as if her body punished her for being so relaxed and risky. Her pulse slowed as she saw no change to the surface of the water.

Just as she sat down, a pressure in her lower abdomen alerted Isla that she needed to use the toilet. Badly. She *did* drink two large mugs of coffee and one bottle of water since she left the dock that morning. Could she wait? She tried, but after three minutes of staring at the water and tapping her foot, she set her book and snack on the bench and went back down the stairs.

After relieving herself, satisfied with an empty bladder, she went back up the stairs. As she became eye-level with the main deck, she could see Jessie had returned.

The damn bird had grabbed the box of snacks and opened the flaps, then knocked the box upside down. The ground was covered in dry food, now becoming soggy from random wet spots.

"You nasty bird!" Isla screamed, waving her hands in the bird's direction.

The bird was so comfortable with humans that at first, it didn't move. But when Isla made a movement as if she was going to kick it, which she wouldn't have anyways, the bird scampered off into the air.

"Gawwwww!" Grabbing the brew in the storage bin near the gull, Isla swept up the mess as best she could. As the last few crumbs came up on her dustbin, a loud splash came from the surface of the waves, followed by a popping noise from a fully-inflated buoyancy compensator.

Chapter 11 - Casper

Despite the awe of the cloudy bottom of the firth, Casper's disappointment filled his body faster than the nitrogen in his tissues. The deep benthics weren't as dark as he expected, but still used his flashlight to examine the rocky corals and critters. He *did* see some nudibranchs, and took pictures of them with his waterproof camera. Not that he could identify them by *Genus species* like an actual scientist in this field could.

There were many slimy-looking animals moving sloth-like along the blades of seagrass, fish poking their heads out of anemones or swarming schools of them migrating above Casper's head. There were larger beasts, and for a panicked moment, Casper though a five-foot seal would bite into his leg. The mammal charged through the water at a terrifying speed, unhindered by the water in its path. The dark canine-like eyes looked the man up and down, then continued swimming past his legs. The tail flipper brushed up against Casper's heel, but he could barely feel it through the layers.

The trip ended when he took mental note of how much oxygen was left in his tank, and he knew it was time to ascend. Using his compass, he found the anchor of the Eimear. Then he took about a minute and half, on the safe side, to reach the surface of the water. He had always been cautious when it came to narcosis, and didn't want to be an idiot.

Biting onto the regulator, Casper swam up to the side of the Eimear. He could see Isla watching him as she lowered the tiny metal ladder down into the waves. The waves pushed him toward the vessel, and he held his hands out so he wouldn't slam into the side. Grabbing the ladder with both hands, he took his time climbing up the slipper rungs. When he had strapped all the gear to his back, chest, and waist, the weight of everything had been difficult to move before the dive. Now, with everything soaked and dripping with saltwater, except for inside the drysuit, he had to use a little bit more muscle to not fall backwards into the waves or face first onto the main deck.

"Here, take my hand," Isla held her arm out as she grabbed his shoulder with her other.

Casper let her support some of the weight as he stepped over the side of the boat and onto the ground. He unclipped the buoyancy compensator and, once Isla was behind him and shouted "I got it", he let the weight slip carefully off his back and shoulders.

"Ahhhhh," he sighed, sitting down on the bench and closing his eyes. The feeling after a dive reminded him of a post-sex orgasm. There was a lot of physical activity, but the end result was blissful exhaustion and relaxation.

"Did you find the sea slug?"

The ecstasy slipped away as Casper thought about how miserable the search went. Looking up at Isla, he saw her bright face waiting for him to respond. She was breaking down his set up, unloosening each tool and hanging up certain ones to dry on a heavy-duty rack in the middle of the deck.

"I found some really cool ones," he said, pulling out his camera from his dry suit pocket but didn't have the energy to power it on, "But not what I was looking for."

"What *are* you looking for?"

There was the question Casper dreaded hearing, and as he thought about how to answer her, he ended up acting as if he didn't hear her. Pulling the diving hood off his head, the cool slow wind blew against his sweaty hair. A chill ran down his scalp and neck, and he noticed a few of dark clouds rolling in.

"Is it going to rain?" He asked, pointing to the incoming weather.

"Probably," Isla laughed, grabbing the hood and setting it on the rack. "I'll let these dry for a bit and we can bring them inside if it starts to pour."

Nodding, Casper began unzipping the drysuit. He didn't unzip it fully beyond his shoulder, and pulled himself out of it. He didn't want to ask Isla for help in case she repeated her former question, and she would be too close to him to ignore.

"Are you hungry?" Isla asked once Casper was free of the diving clothes.

"I can make some lunch," he strapped in the oxygen tanks so they wouldn't bump around onboard. "I don't mind cooking, if I'm allowed to use the stove."

"If that's what you prefer," Isla shrugged, "I'll be up here."

As Casper walked toward the stairs, he paused and looked back at her. "Do you want me to cook you something?"

"Och, no thank you," she let out a heavily-accented laugh, different from her usual clear pronunciation, "I ate before you came up."

"I'll see you in about an hour," he said, stepping down, "For dive number two."

In the kitchenette, he cooked up some fish and mixed vegetables. Stomach growling, he hurried as fast as he could to make the food edible. Once prepared, he devoured the hot meal as fast as possible. While doing so, he flipped through his notebook.

The notes were in his sister's handwriting, and while most of it was clear and legible, there were parts that were smeared or erased. Even though Casper had studied the notebook, front to back, about a million times, there were still hints and secrets he discovered when he came back to the book.

Bella Shaw was an explorer in the American continents. Just think of Indiana Jones, except a tiny woman who used more wit than whip to find long lost items. Her interest began while she studied archeology at New York University, and she went on many excavations around the world. Then she was hired by a non-profit research team to find objects lost in the Caribbean waters during the Golden Age of Piracy.

When Bella had told Casper and their parents about her new job, they were both excited and doubtful of the employers. Casper had believed all old treasure had already been dug up and discovered, and placed in museums or auctioned by rich people. Then Bella and her coworkers were in the newspapers about unearthing treasure lost by Howell Davis. She even wrote a book on it.

Many other interesting lost objects were found, and Bella was quickly becoming one of the best treasure hunters globally. Then she paired up with an explorer named Liam Martinez, and she didn't come home for the holidays. Her body was found on a deserted sandy beach of Barbados, with signs of head trauma and strangulation.

Casper doesn't know what most people would do. What he did, though, was retrieve all of her belongings and research from her office in New York City and bring it back to Boston. He knew her company would come asking for her notes, so when they claimed that her research was company policy, handed them over after making photocopies of each page. The one thing he held onto was her notebook. The company dismissed it, saying it must have gotten lost in the Carribean, or whoever murdered her took it. No, she simply hadn't brought it with her on the last trip. So she knew something was up the days leading to her death.

There was so much information on each page, words scribbled small from top to bottom and in each margin. The last few pages were empty, but the notes leading up to the end suggested a new lead. Scotland. Where a pirate's ship was attacked by British soldiers, and treasure was lost deep in the abyssal waters between the west coast of Scotland and the east coast of Ireland.

Further investigation by Casper led him to believe, due to the currents, the treasure would be right in the firth. He could be wrong as there was no real scientific way in his investigations. He consulted history books and records, telling museums he was a graduate student of history, anthropology, even English, anything plausible to grant him access to primary sources.

None of the sources know who the pirate was on the ship destroyed in the Autumn of 1763. The British man-o-war had followed the pirate and his crew for a day down from the Lewis and Harris island, far north of Scotland before attacking. Some historians claim it wasn't a pirate at all but a former Jacobite, despite the last rising being almost twenty years prior. People remembered, Casper read, and still held resentment in their hearts against the English king. Many well-known pirates were former Jacobites, but they ruled in the Carribeans and along the east coast of North American. Casper knew this from speaking with his sister, as she followed the historical tracks of William Kidd and Alexander Dalzeel. Also, smugglers were called pirates, and the British outlawed many items that the people of the world desired.

While searching for treasure was exciting and could prove bountiful, part of Casper expected to dreg up an ancient, disgusting crate of whiskey. In reality, Casper didn't care what he found, as long as he found it first.

Chapter 12 - Kelsey

One of Kelsey's treasured feelings in the world is the anticipation of departure. As he watches his crew carry crates along the gangways from the docks to the Crooked Stock's main deck, the feeling rises and he can't wait to open the white sails and head south. It's been many months since he's felt the warm sunlight of France, and they ran out of champagne, three weeks ago, and he was thirsty for expensive taste.

Not that the wine Laird Thomas had given him wasn't expensive, but the Scottish brand didn't hit the way the champagne did. Imagining the fruity light aroma of alcoholic bubbles brought back memories of vast fields of golden wheat, insects buzzing at all hours of the day and night, a woman with long black hair looking back at Kelsey with a smile that said *Chase me, I dare you.* It was the same smile he saw when his son laughed at the crude jokes from the crew, or when his son remembered how to do a bowline knot correctly.

"Where ye want this?"

Looking at the gangway closest, Kelsey saw Mateo and another of the crew hoisting a long wooden chest. Though most of it looked plain, the lock in front expressed intricate metalwork, iron weaving around each other into the crest of Laird Thomas's house. The only key was on Kelsey's hip, tucked in a pocket where all his other keys were collected on a metal ring. The only other person who knew where the key was happened to be the Laird.

"In my cabin," Kelsey ran his index finger over the top of the chest as the two men carried it by, and a sliver caught in his skin. Though he made no indication of the tiny pain as he brought his finger up to view. The infetismal slice of wood stood out at an angle, and around it was the promise of blood.

"Was that what the Laird gave you?" David asked, coming alongside his father.

"It is," Kelsey nodded, dropping his hand to his side and looking out at the docks. The early morning fog concealed most of the town, but the faint black steeples of the buildings poked out through the white mist. The other ships and docks appeared to disappear into the fog, and sailors and merchants from other vessels materialized and faded as they went about their duties. The scene was eerie, and Kelsey was eager to depart.

"Where are we taking it?" David asked, poking at a sack of grain that hadn't been brought down to the hold yet.

"Taking what, son?"

"The Laird's chest?"

"Oh," the captain thought about the parchment Thomas had given him, the instructions inked out for Kelsey in case he forgot. He could never forget his old friend's request, though. "We're bringing it home for a bit."

"Is there a buyer in Le Havre?" David grabbed a bottle of ale as two crewmembers carried an open crate past him.

"Yes," Kelsey loved the child, but felt particularly annoyed at the boy's innocent investigation at present. "Go take that sack down below."

"Yes, sir!" The boy, eager to please his father, captain, king of his universe, picked up the heavy sack. The bag was almost the size of the boy, but probably weighed more than him. Living a sailor's life, he was conditioned enough for heavy lifting, but still was just a child.

"Remember," Kelsey shouted in a playful tone, trying not to laugh, "Use your arse, not your back!"

Taking a new approach, David squatted down and wrapped his arms around the sack. With the weight close to his chest, the boy managed to lift the sack up as he stood to his full height.

"Good man!" Kelsey clapped the boy on the shoulder, almost causing the boy to topple over. "Now bring it down."

The boy did as told, taking his time with the stairs. A few other members of the crew hollered at him for taking so damn slow, but most meant well as the men had a love for him. Partially due to him being the offspring of Kelsey Vargas, but also because he tried his darndest to keep up and carry his weight, even if his tiny muscles couldn't handle it. Like right now.

"Everything is down below," Mateo said after stopping in front of Kelsey. "Tide will be going out soon. Shall we make way?"

Taking in a deep breath, Kelsey took one last look at the gloomy fog of the Outer Hebrides of Scotland. "Let's go."

A number of men of the crew climbed up the ropes on both sides of the ship, their calloused hands pulling the thick threads down their body. Some wore boots while others preferred bare soles, and they pushed the ropes down as they carried their bodies up toward the masts. In a few minutes, the mainsail relaxed downward from the ties, and there was a small billowing from the seabreeze. The current assisted in bringing the ship out of the inlet, as well as a smaller boat, and Kelsey kept his hands loose on the circular helm as he directed the bow away from the land.

The fog didn't lift, and seemed to thicken as the bumpy brisk seas surrounded the Crooked Stock. Mornings were usually cold, quiet, and gray. It was one of the reasons why Kelsey wanted to get an early start, even if every man on his crew were expecting an afternoon start. They invested their time, money, and liver the previous night believing they would be allowed to sleep past the rising sun with one or two women draped around their alcohol-infused bodies.

Once speaking to Laird Thomas, though, Kelsey was eager to leave British territory. His crew trusted him when he woke their asses up hours before dawn, which was shortly after his return to the tavern from the castle. The first thing he did was speak with Mateo, commanding his trusted second to take three of their most trusted sailors and go pick up a wooden chest from the castle's stables. Then

Kelsey woke the rest of the men and told them they must begin their leave earlier than expected. They all listened, but all the same, most men grumbled from sleep-deprivation and hangovers.

Kelsey knew his men deserved a few nights of rest, but once he spoke to Thomas, circumstances changed. He also was unable to refuse an old friend, much less the Laird. Even if Thomas hadn't been nobility, Kelsey would have helped him. It didn't really matter, the *what ifs* and *what thens*. All that mattered now was getting down the Atlantic, through the seas between Ireland and Scotland, and across the channels of England.

Chapter 13 - Isla

The rain did come, but Isla made sure all of the damp scuba diving equipment was stored neatly in the bins before the water fell to the deck. There had been a few orange cracker crumbs that Isla had missed when cleaning the mess before, but they dissolved and spilled away as the raindrops arrived. Just as the wind picked up and the rain fell harder, Isla checked all status at the helm and went down below.

The smell of garlic, onions, and cilantro curled up the stairs and around Isla's face. She closed the hatch at the top of the steps, which kept the stairs dry and the rain out. The aroma grew and as she walked across to her bed, she saw Casper pouring a serving of food onto a plate.

"That smells delicious," she said, hanging her raincoat up on a hook by the water closet.

"I cooked up the stirfry," Casper said, placing his plate on the small table. "I know you said you weren't hungry but I made extras."

"I'll eat the rest," Isla went to the kitchen counter and loaded a plate up with noodles and vegetables. Her eyes watered a little from the onions, but she didn't mind. Setting the plate down on the table, she turned and grabbed two crystal glasses and a bottle of whiskey from the cupboard.

"Are you still up to your second dive?" She asked as she poured a small amount of the amber alcohol into each glass.

"Of course!" Casper gave her a look as if she was mad. "A little rain won't get in my way. It can't!"

"I understand," she sat down and dug her fork into the noodles, twisting the edible strings around the prongs. "The currents will be strong, though. The wind doesn't help."

"If I always waited for the weather to be appropriate," Casper picked up his glass, "I'd never go under."

He brought the glass to his lips and tilted his head back, throwing all the liquid into his mouth. Isla tried not to stare as the American didn't seem affected by the burn down his throat. She was used to foreigners acting high and mighty around the national alcohol but then choking from a few sips. This man made no change in expression from the slight frustrated look he held since his last dive.

"You said you saw some slugs," Isla said, taking a sip of her whiskey, "What kind?"

At that moment, Casper shoved a large fork full of noodles into his mouth. He tried speaking, but it was incoherent, so he closed his lips and gestured to his lips. Isla raised an eyebrow as she looked down at her own dish. He was an odd one, she thought, or just didn't want to talk about his research.

"There were some Aeolids," he finally said, patting his lips with a napkin, "The ones that have the cerata on their back."

"The little spines with the stinging cells, right?" Isla could feel her face light up, but she couldn't help feeling happy talking about marine animals. Or at least, not salmon.

"Yes," Casper poured himself another glass of whiskey, but Isla reached her hand out.

"If you're diving again," she said, "You shouldn't drink more than one glass."

He paused before resting the bottle down and sliding it toward her. "You're right. I completely forgot. I just don't drink Scottish whiskey often, so I try to enjoy it when I can."

"Could've fooled me," Isla laughed, piercing an onion slice with her utensil, "You chugged that first glass like it was juice."

Shrugging, Casper finished his meal and brought his plate to the sink.

"So are you looking for Aeolids or Dorids?" Isla asked, not wanting their science conversation to end.

"Uh, dorid?" It sounded like a question, the way Casper answered. As if he didn't know. "Dorid. It's white, mostly white, actually."

"And you aren't collecting?" As much as Isla didn't want to pry, she felt herself slip into the role as academic professor, eager to question the scientific method of her students.

"No, only photos and documentation," Casper said, his words barely audible over the running sink faucet and the heavy rain overhead.

"There's a lot of white Dorid nudibranchs," Isla finished eating her food but didn't stand, "Along the west coast of Scotland."

"Yeah?" This response was less like a question and more like a challenge, as if he was saying *Are you really questioning my expertise?* The word also sparked a warm feeling inside Isla's abdomen, and she was more tempted to continue.

"If you really want to know if you have the right species," she said, grabbing her plate and bringing it to the counter by the sink, "You need to collect specimens and bring them to a lab, and perform genetic analysis on them."

There was a silence as Isla waited for the diver to respond, and when he didn't say anything, she looked up at him. He was slowly drying off his plate, and slow about putting it in the cupboard.

"I didn't mean offense," Isla said, stepping away from him to give him space, "It's just been a while since I debated methodology."

"I really don't feel comfortable debating," Casper said, turning to look at her, and their eyes met. "I know some researchers do."

"I apologize," Isla felt heat rise in her cheeks, "I just am not used to field work, surprisingly."

"Tell me," Casper's face softened as he took her plate and began rinsing it, "What do you do in your lab? Your curiosity is infectious, and now I want to know about you."

Grinning, Isla sat back down at the table and watched him clean then dry her plate. With his back to her, she could look at him shamelessly. And she did, noticing the tight fit of his fleece sweater, his broad shoulders and muscular back. A small part of her had been disappointed that he hadn't worn a wetsuit, which would have required him to be shirtless. She would've witnessed how defined his muscles were. Though the Scottish waters are cold, and he wouldn't have been able to dive without the proper dry suit to keep him warm.

"Fine," Isla poured another thin line of amber at the bottom of her glass, "Let me tell you about salmon."

Chapter 14 - Casper

Warnings signs blasted in Casper's head, but when he had met Isla's questioning gaze, the blinking mental alarms were suppressed. WHen he told her he didn't like debating, he knew he was lying. He enjoyed arguing, when the situation was appropriate, but he couldn't risk her learning about his true identity. Still, a warmth expanded throughout his chest and reached in between his legs. At the same time, he felt his whole body melt into a puddle when he looked at her.

Now, back in his second dive, Casper's whole body was rigid as an icicle, which was what his skin felt like despite the dry suit. Even though he was diving in the same location as earlier, the current mixed with colder waters, and the temperature below the surface had decreased. The thermocline had shocked him on the first dive, but every ten seconds it felt as if he passed through a new layer of freezing saltwater. His lungs were taking up more oxygen as he gasped more often, unable to quickly calm his brain after each change in temperature. Just as he thought it couldn't get any colder, another underwater wave rushed over him and goosebumps shot along his body.

The physical struggle made Casper's search difficult. It was already hard enough with the dim light and the altered vision from being in saltwater. What light there was, from above or his flashlight, hit the bottom differently than it would in the air above the surface. Different medium, different view of the world.

Following his compass, Casper found the exact coordinates penned down in his sister's notebook. In the spot, there was a large rock about seven feet high from the seafloor. The rock was covered in hard corals, barnacles, and other strange marine flora and fauna To Casper, it didn't look different from the rest of the floor, but he kicked his flippers a little so he was floating right next to the rock. His flashlight revealed the naturally-occuring details on the hard surface, where the rock underneath fused together, and where the solid homes of tiny animals began and ended. To any authentic marine biologist, he or she would be able to envision a crowded city of diversity, and ecosystem where all animals and plants played an important role on this rock, which was only a bit taller than Casper himself. To him, this rock was a location scribbled in the notebook, so it was important enough to explore.

Using one gloved hand, Casper brushed his hands around waving corals and floating seagrasses so he could see behind and under their shadows. Crabs scuttered away, fish went wide-eyed and hid. Casper didn't know what he was looking for, but he knew something had to be here. His sister was never wrong, even when dead.

Searching the rock top to bottom, Casper didn't find anything man made. Another cold current passed around him, and he glanced at his oxygen levels. He had to return soon. There was nothing here, but there had to be. He had faith in his sister, so he concluded that *he* simply couldn't find whatever was here to be found. There were other locations to search, but why *this* one?

As he turned to head back to the anchor, the glow of his flashlight ran across the floor under him. Something caught his eye, and he paused. Took a deep breath. And reached out.

Dusting off some sand and marine weeds, Casper uncovered a reddish-brown object. Carefully, he pulled it out from the crevices between two rocks and brought it up to his goggles. It was a rusted piece of metal, a ring that was fixed through a small hole of a flat piece of metal that was shaped like a sun. It was as wide as his palm, and layers of the rust fell away from being handle.

As gentle as possible in his heightened excitement, Casper opened one of his little pouches and placed the metal piece inside. Closing the bag tightly, he quickly looked around for any other metal objects. Satisfied with the discovery, he focused on getting back to the anchor and up to the boat before he lost feeling in his fingers. He already couldn't feel his lips.

✳✳

"You seem in a better mood," Isla said after they settled downstairs for the evening. "Does that mean—"

"Yes," Casper nodded, grinning, "I found it."

"The sea slug?" She asked, letting him pour more of the whiskey now that he was finished diving.

"Mhmmm," he poured more whiskey than he should have, but he didn't care for he wanted to celebrate; his sister was never wrong, and he almost gave up on her.

"Do you have a picture?" Isla asked, and he noticed she was preparing a set of clothes to take into the bathroom with her. "I'd like to see it."

"Actually, my camera needs to charge," he gestured to the tiny waterproof camera that was attached to a power bank on his bed, the orange light blinking. "But afterwards, yeah."

"So should we stay here?" Isla asked, holding the clothes to her chest. "Tomorrow?"

"Oh, no," he said, trying not to notice the lacey pair of blue panties on top of her clothes. It was barely noticeable, but he could see part of it sticking out. "Now that I've confirmed the species is here, I need to go to the other locations and do the same."

"Oh, alright," she turned and stepped to the bathroom door, "I'm washing up. Do you need anything before I do?"

Shaking his head, Casper watched as she went into the tiny room and closed the door. He heard the lock click, and then the faucet turn on. Right, there wasn't a shower on board, so any cleaning they had to do was by washcloth. It was so not modern, but Casper wouldn't complain. Sure, the captain was interested in who he was and what he did, but it was innocent. She wasn't a threat.

After cleaning the table and kitchen sink, Casper went to his bed and laid down. He didn't feel like looking at the notebook, but a part of him said he had to. So he pulled the notebook out and read through the notes for tomorrow. Stuffed in the bin under his bed, the rusty metal piece was wrapped in plastic and placed in a box under his clothes. There wasn't really anywhere safer to hide it, but also he didn't really think Isla would go through his things. As curious as she was, she also didn't seem suspicious or concerned. He didn't know what he would do if she was, as he liked her. She was hot, but not only that, she had this presence about her that made him want to laugh. She was always in an upbeat mood, and she kept asking questions. As much as Casper knew how dangerous it would be for her to find out his true intentions, he had this instinctual urge to tell her everything.

Chapter 15 - Kelsey

David was a sweet child, despite the life forced upon him. The thing is, though, Kelsey could do better by his son. The child could have a better education, tutors for seven different subjects. His skills could be refined, allowing him opportunities in noble society. He could continue the family name, perhaps grow the family business to the glory it once was.

The boy was watching a group of seagulls circling around one of the masts. One dipped into the wind while another sat on the horizontal wooden post. Kelsey walked up to his son and leaned against the banister, the same position as the boy.

"Got tired of that new book?" Kelsey asked. If there was one thing he did right by David, he taught him how to read and write.

"I finished it," David responded, his voice small. "I didn't understand most of it."

"That's alright," Kelsey grabbed an apple from his pocket and handed it to the boy. "Here, got an extra one from the galley. He said you skipped your meal?"

The boy's face brightened when he saw the red apple. He took it with both hands and smiled. "I appreciate it."

"You ill?" Kelsey asked, observing the healthy colour of the boy's face, the red tinge in his cheeks.

Shaking his head, David bit into the apple. "I wanted to finish reading."

Kelsey laughed and scanned the deck. "You remind me of your mother. She would skip mealtime, teatime, even important gatherings just to hold a book open."

Though he wasn't looking directly at David, Kelsey could tell the boy was listening intently. Though it hurt to talk about Antona, Kelsey knew it was important for David to know who his mother was. Or at least, who she was to Kelsey.

"What was her favorite book?" David asked, speaking with apple bits in his mouth.

"Oh, she read *Gulliver's Travels* about three times," Kelsey grinned, remembering the old copy in the reading room of where they used to live, before Aimée passed away. "She read *Robinson Crusoe* once, and like you, didn't quite enjoy it."

"They both are about adventure," David said, pausing the apple in front of his lips, "But aren't the same."

"I wouldn't know," Kelsey looked down at his son's face, "As I don't read stories. Glad you do, though. Passes the time incredibly, except now you have nothing to read for the next few weeks."

The boy looked a little embarrassed, but Kelsey slapped him playfully on the shoulder.

"Not a bad thing, you reading so quick," Kelsey said, resting his hand on the boy's shoulder and looking off at the sea. "Just means you're smart. You'd do well back home."

"Father," David had a confused expression, "Ruben said men who read too much are stuffy and landlubbers. I don't want to be like that. And I think I know a lot about the sea."

"Oh," Kelsey glanced over at the fat man scaling the ropes toward the topmast, "People have their thoughts on reading, and some are envious of great talent. While the educated shouldn't put the uneducated people beneath them, those that are uneducated shouldn't hate us."

"If you're educated," David asked, his eyebrows still furrowed, "Why aren't we still in France?"

"France isn't the only place for well-read individuals," Kelsey laughed. "And those who read are as useful on the sea as they are in buildings."

David became quiet, as if his childish brain needed time to process this adult information. Pulling his hand off David's shoulder, Kelsey turned around to face the sea.

"Did I ever tell you about my childhood?" Kelsey asked, knowing he's told this story at least a dozen times.

"No," David copied his father's position: elbows on the banister, one leg bent forward and the other straightened back, like a lunge.

"Well, I grew up with more educated folk," Kelsey explained, watching the waves on the water. "Though the town where I lived, there were many men who worked with their hands. Sailors, builders, farmers. Even if they didn't know more than one language, or they couldn't recite poetry, they had wisdom. Tales that explained the world."

"That was in America, right?" David asked, looking up at the grey sky.

"Portobelo," Kelsey smiled, remembering the tropical warm air, the thick moisture that hovered over his skin. "It was like most port cities you've seen, but vibrant. There were people from all over who sold their wares there. That's how the Vargas family became well known in Spain, strangely."

"Why was it strange?"

"The Vargas merchants did well in Spain," Kelsey shrugged, "But when your great-grandfather grew his wealth in the Portobelo, the number of his associates in Spain grew."

"Was it because they thought he was brave?" David asked. "Since he went across the ocean and survived?"

"Perhaps," Kelsey raised an eyebrow at his son, grinning. "Perhaps not. Remember, people sometimes cross the oceans because they're forced to, not because they want to."

"Was grandfather forced?"

"No." There was a pause before Kelsey continued his story. "While I enjoyed my childhood there, I found I enjoyed working away from buildings and crowds and all the details of a businessman on land. Even when I transported goods across the French border for your great uncle,

I longed to set sail. I can wear what I want here, and I don't have to carry any airs about me."

"Except for the air of captain," David said, straightforward, and Kelsey smiled again.

"Yes, of course," Kelsey stood up straight and sighed. "I also enjoy being able to leave a place whenever I need. My home is always with me. After the British destroyed Portobelo, I lost my home. Then when your mother died, that was a different kind of loss that you will understand one day. But I couldn't stay there."

"Um," David threw his apple core overboard, "I thought we left because you upset Lord Olivernon and he was going to kill you."

"Yes, that had a play in my decision to leave," Kelsey tilted his head to the side and squeezed his eyes shut for a moment. "Now that the bastard has finally died, we may return without worry of retaliation."

"Will home look the same?" David asked, bouncing on the balls of his feet as he watched the apple bob on the surface of the water. "When we return?"

"No," Kelsey was sure of this. "Much has happened in the last few years. Yet we shall work with what we're given."

Chapter 16 - Isla

The boat always needed tending, so while keeping an eye on the waters, Isla let the music blast on the stereo and scrubbed the wooden floorboards of the main deck. She could see the red and white scuba diving flag bob on the surface from where she was, and kept an eye on her watch.

Casper had just dove under five minutes prior, so Isla wasn't planning on seeing him for another forty-five minutes or so. He was eager to hop over into the water, despite how cold it was. It's funny how Isla enjoys the ocean so much, but can't stand how frigid the temperature is of the Scottish seas. She never enjoyed swimming past her waist, and even then that was too much to handle. Occasionally, she did dip her hand into the water by the docks, just to refuel her soul.

The lyrics belting in Steven Tyler's voice slowed, something Isla hadn't predicted while she sang along during her mindless chores. The station seemed to cut in and out, play the song clearly for a few more seconds, and then a popping sound came from the old chunk of electric wiring and silver plastic.

"No, no, no!" Isla let the mop drop out of her hands as she rushed over to the sheltered hull and knelt down to the ground. At first, she kept her fingers away from the stereo to check if it was safe to touch. No smoke came out from cracks, so she flicked the power switch to OFF.

It was bound to die eventually, being built and bought in the early nineties. It had been a prize won at the townhall's weekly bingo game, which still happened every Thursday night. Isla remembered her mother refusing to place the large ugly stereo system in the house, so Isla's father kept it in the boat. He thought it added character, and didn't think once about upgrading to an iPod with speakers. He still carried a flip phone up until he died, and was now rotting somewhere in the house with the rest of his outdated mess.

Pulling the stereo away from the wall, Isla tried finding the reason for its demise. It probably was just old and worn out. Since being brought onboard, the only time it was shut off was at night. If anything, its death was overdue.

There was no water damage that Isla could see. The wall it had been pressed up against had a darker appearance from lack of sun exposure. The wooden boards making up the small enclosure around the hull were built close together, as well as the floorboards. Except one small plank positioned directly under where the stereo had rested for almost three decades.

Isla's eyebrows furrowed as she examined the loose floorboard, and she slid her fingernail into the crack and pulled the slab up and to the side. Inside the secret compartment was a plastic ziplock bag filled with stuff.

Looking at her watch, Isla estimated Casper would surface in thirty-five minutes so she had time. She pulled the plastic bag out of the hole and realized there were papers held inside. Turning it over in her hands, she didn't have to open the bag to read the first message. A large blue sticky note inside the bag read "Urchin, do not show anyone these. It's too dangerous to trust"

The last part of the note seemed odd, as if whoever wrote it truly meant 'don't trust anyone' but it also felt as if the sentence wasn't finished. Also, Isla knew who wrote it.

Isla's nickname as a child was 'urchin', not because she was a poor child who roamed dirty in the streets, but because she used to collect sea urchins like rocks and bring them home. She would collect the spiny balls of life, put them in her metal pail, and fill the bathtub up with water. She did this about three times until she learned she was the reason why they died, since the freshwater from the tub made them sick. The guilt she held was terrible, but her parents found the ordeal hilarious. Thus, the nickname sprouted and stuck all the way through college. And to now.

Why would he hide these here? What if I never found them? Isla thought about what her father experienced the days leading up to his death, and the familiar sinking hole of sorrow and heartache filled her chest and mind. She thought about all the times he called her and she purposely ignored him, busy with her work. The times she did answer, he would almost beg her to come visit, but never begged, so it came out as "I need help solving this puzzle I have" or "Your brain and talents are needed back home." Reading this note made Ilsa wonder if there was a point to his slipping hold on reality. Perhaps he wasn't mad, and he was in trouble.

Opening the ziplock top, Isla reached in and pulled one of the paper out. Some of them looked old, stained yellow with time. Some were in her father's hand, others unfamiliar to her. She began reading the first line, *"The Genealogy Society of Scotland: Chapter of the West Coast—"*

A violent splashing erupted from the surface of the water, and the telltale popping of a buoyancy compensator suggested Casper had completed his dive. Isla hurried to place the paper back into the bag, place the bag back into the hole, slide the wood back into place, and push the boombox back into the corner. When she reached the side of the boat, she couldn't see Casper's expression as his lips were curled around the regulator, his eyes hidden beyond his foggy goggles.

Lowering the ladder, Isla felt her hands shaking. Her mind wasn't here and now, itching to get back to the documents and find out what her father was hiding. She wondered if there was a method to the madness cluttering the house, and she had simply been ignoring to start investigating a really important mystery.

"Where were you?" Casper spit out his regulator and was ripping his equipment off before Ilsa could help. The tone of his voice was sharp like the biting sea water, and Isla knew it was her fault. "I don't mean to be rude, but I have paid you to take care of me, which means watch the surface for when I return and help me get back on the boat."

Silent, Isla's mind flipped through the proper responses. She didn't know what to say as she had never felt or acted so careless in her life. A part of her wanted to throw her hands up, turn the boat toward shore, and throw him off. She didn't need the money, and she could just pack up her shit and go *home*. Back to the university.

"Isla!" Casper raised his voice, his face closer to hers, sounding more concerned since she wasn't saying anything. "Do you understand that you are in charge of my safety?"

"Y-yes," for the first time in her entire professional career, her bottom lip quivered, and she bit it to control the shaking, "I'm sorry. It won't happen again."

The diver paused as he stepped closer, watching her face. Isla wanted to run downstairs and hide, feeling hot tears cloud her vision, but she tried blinking them back and swallowing her sadness down and out of her throat.

"Is everything okay?" Casper asked, reaching his gloved hand out and placing it on her shoulder. "What's wrong?"

"Nothing," Isla stepped to the side, away from his hand, and reached for the zipper on his drysuit. "Let me help you."

The zipper opened the drysuit from the abdomen to the shoulder, and then a bit on the upper back. Casper climbed out of the suit and set it up to dry, along with his fins, hood, and gloves. Isla strapped the other items, taking the time to clear her throat and mind. Her cheeks burned, wondering how poorly Casper thought of her. Would he cancel the second charter trip once they reached land?

During dinner, which was earlier since Casper surfaced fifteen minutes than expected, Isla cooked up box macaroni and cheese for both of them.

"Not the healthiest," Isla said, setting two warm bowls on the table, "But sometimes it hits the right spot on a cold day."

"I thought this was an American thing," Casper laughed, grabbing a spoonful of cheesy noodles. "The whole processed food thing."

"Have you seen the way we eat in the UK?" Isla had poured them glasses of water, not wanting to touch the whiskey for fear her inhibitions would loosen. She didn't want to at last talk about her father, much less to a stranger.

"I guess you needed some soul food?" Casper asked, giving her a careful glance, a hidden smirk playing on his lips.

Sighing, Isla swirled a noddle around the bottom of her bowl with her spoon. "I do."

"You haven't taken a bite, though."

Her eyes flickered up to Casper's, and he was watching her while he ate. Picking up a spoonful, she brought the food to her lips. His eyes followed, not once looking away. She licked her lips, and wrapped them around the spoon, pulling the food into her mouth. Yes, the artificial cheese was delicious and filled her with joy. But it wasn't the cause of the spreading warmth in her abdomen and between her legs. It was the way Casper's eyes examined her, the way he looked like he craved what he saw, wondering if he should pounce.

"Did you find anything this time?" She finally asked, and his eyes fell to his empty bowl.

"No, not at this location," he said, twirling his spoon around his bowl. "Tomorrow I hope will prove successful."

"For the next trip," Isla asked, "WIll we come back to these three spots?"

"Not to the one yesterday," he ran a hand through his hair, and it fell back against his forehead. "I'm thinking we might return to this one."

"Mhmmm," less sultry, Isla shoved a large spoonful into her mouth. "Sounds good to me."

As she finished her meal, she watched as Casper cleaned his bowl, grabbed a set of clothes from his bunk, and locked himself in the water closet. She imagined him taking his shirt and pants off, and she wondered if he wore undergarments. The last time she saw a man without clothes had been Billie, which was…

Damn, Isla thought to herself as she crossed her restless legs, *It's been years since I've been laid.*

Chapter 17 - Casper

The latest incident with Isla gave Casper chills, and he thought about the whole afternoon while lying in his bed, trying to sleep. She hadn't been present for when he had surfaced. He could've been out on the sea for minutes wasting oxygen and time, and if he had run out of the little oxygen he had left, he would have to change to his snorkel. The simple piece of equipment is great for swimming on the surface, but what if a strong current pulled him under the waves? So many things could go wrong in seconds, and Isla wouldn't have known.

But the thing that sent shivers down his spine more than her careless work ethic is the way she made him feel during dinner. She had evoked a heavy thirst deep in his gut, especially when she silently prompted him to watch her envelop her spoon with her lips. Oh, she *knew* what she was doing, despite all other attempts at a professional relationship. Casper sensed that the fine line between business and customer was looking more like the crashing waves surrounding the boat.

He had pressed the woman into talking about her personal life, but it would have been hard not to with her sudden change in attitude and the obvious tears filling her eyes. In the three days Casper had known Isla, he had rarely seen her frown. If she wasn't smiling, her lips would be set in a straight line during times of concentration. But never upset. It was only human to ask her what was wrong.

The other reason for why he was so pissed after his last dive was because he surfaced empty handed. Finding the metal piece yesterday had set him up for excitement, which led him to fall harder into disappointment. There were no large rocks to search, but the vast sea floor with the usual critters. Nothing reflected light except the shiny scales on fish, or marine eyes peering out from behind coral.

He had a feeling that he should go back to where he found the metal piece. That would be the most obvious decision. Why would he travel further away from the location he had success? Well, because of the notebook. The notes weren't clear, parts missing, but the notes referenced historical oceanographical data from the late 1700s, recorded data on dredging trips along the seafloor, and the routes the British had taken during the 1760s. All this information was not collected in the notebook, so Casper couldn't confirm if the notes were correct. His sister could have read a table wrong or mixed up information, leading readers of her notes in the wrong direction. But then he found the metal piece, and decided to stop doubting Bella's research efforts.

A soft snore came from across the cabin, and Casper craned his head to see Isla's sleeping form in her bed. She had fallen asleep fast, and hadn't stirred once. She slept in the clothes she had worn that day, only changing the next morning into new clothes. The idea of the poor hygiene would turn Casper off, but he understood the life of a charter boat. He went on a few multi-day dive trips before, and while they were slightly nicer than Isla's arrangements, they weren't much better. Just like this trip, Casper had changed his clothes frequently. He didn't like to sleep in the same clothes he wore all day, and he liked to change his socks at least three times a day. It was something he picked up from Bella after she came back from an excavation in the Amazonian jungle. One important rule: keep your feet dry.

On any other dive trip, Casper's toes would stretch out in sandals. But this was the Northern Atlantic, and both day and nights required socks and warm boots. Of course, the blanket weighing him done currently was warm enough for his toes to wiggle in the wool socks. The pillow under his head was very comfortable, which was why he couldn't fall asleep. Well, one of the reasons.

He liked his pillows more firm, like at the bed and breakfast on shore. He knew Isla most likely paid a higher price for these pillows, hoping to provide as much comfort to divers as she could. Not everyone enjoyed the comfy lifestyle. Somehow, sometime, Casper was able to fall into a sleep deep enough to ful him for the next day.

The first dive proved to be somewhat successful.

This last location had towers of kelp, appearing similar to the kelp forests off the coast of Central California. The greenish vines wove around each other, forming a trunk of sorts. Leaves sprouted off, but if Casper knew anything about marine biology, these towers of life were not plants. Similar to the corals on the rocky bottom, fish and other animals inhabited the tree-like projections. Casper had to be more cautious as there were more spots for seals and large fish to hide, and he didn't want to surprise any animals that had the ability to bite him.

Letting small increments of air out of the buoyancy compensator, Casper reached the bottom of the kelp seascape in a few minutes. It wasn't deep like yesterday, but the "foliage" surrounding him caused light to be dim, so he still used his flashlight. Just as the two previous days, he scanned the floor for anything that looked made by humans. After fifteen minutes, Casper was floating about three feet above the seafloor, looking slightly above his eye level with his light. He almost missed it, his light running over it. His brain processed what he had found, and he placed his gloved hand quick against the sandyrock below his chest. The slight current dragged against him, and he felt a little dizzy from stopping suddenly.

Pointing the light under him, he could see the sand had been disturbed and was floating around in front of his goggles. The sand settled down back to where it belonged, and as the water cleared, the round silver object was all Casper could see.

The American wrapped his clumsy fingers around the object and pulled it away from the ground. A long chain came with it, and with close inspection, he could see it was a locket. Though, it didn't look as if he had been rusting away under the sea for roughly three hundred years.

Casper used the last thirty minutes picking the area for other treasures, but he only brought the locket back to the surface.

Chapter 18 - Kelsey

One day into the voyage and the Crooked Stock needed repairs. A crewmember was doing a routine inspection of the foundation and discovered rot in one of the walls of the storage room. Even if it might cause no issue for the next few days to France, Kelsey didn't like to mess with evil possibilities. After speaking with Mateo, he ordered for the ship to be grounded on the closest beach.

While Sotland consisted of many coastal cliffs, there were many sandy inlets. As the crew worked with the favorable high tide, they cussed and shouted orders to each other. Together, they tied the ship to nearby trees, sweating and straining legs and back muscles. Once everyone was confident that the ship wouldn't move, they assisted Mariano, the carpenter, as he surveyed the damage and planned repairs.

"We have the supplies for it," Mariano said, taking his small glasses off and wiping the lenses clean. "It'll take me the day, though."

"We're in no rush," Kelsey observed the rot, trying not to show his disdain at the soften wooden panels. "I'll give Jasper, Ruben, and Joey and to assist you."

"I have to say," Mariano squinted at the panels, putting his glasses back on, "i'm surprised this has gone unnoticed for so long. This should have been brought to my attention some time ago."

"That's what I was thinking," Kelsey put his hands on his hips, mustering the gust to sound authoritative. "We just changed the men's duties, so it must have been overlooked by the previous man assigned."

Wordless, Kelsey pressed two fingers against the rot and felt a shiver run up his spine as water squeezed through.

"Best if I start, captain," Mariano unrolled a leather case of tools.

"Thank you, Mariano," Kelsey gave a short nod before heading to where the men waited further up the beach.

A small camp had been set up as the men knew the repairs would take some time. There was a fire and a medium-sized roasting pig rotating above the flames. The men were drinking and laughing, leering and joking with one another. All except on: Filipe.

Filipe was not a bad man, or at least if he was, Kelsey had no knowledge of the sailor's sins. While each man had their one indiscretions and mistakes, Kelsey generally did not hire men that possessed the enjoyment to hurt others. Most captains didn't care who they hired, only if they worked hard and didn't cause problems. Kelsey didn't feel right working with cold-blooded murderers, just those who killed because they had to. Those who fought for their lives and families.

Filipe always seemed to border that line. He spoke ill of women, and while Kelsey never directly heard such hatred from the man, gossip circled back to the captain of the acts Filipe wished to do or had done to the opposite sex. When on land, Filipe was the one who caused brawl fights and the law to step in. Each time, Kelsey had to deal with these issues and help Filipe, either with coin or his own carefully-chosen words.

Now, Filipe sat with the group surrounding the roasting pig, but he wasn't smiling. The moment Kelsey set eyes on the round middle-aged man, the same age as Kelsey, Filipe's glare shot down to the sand between his feet. Kelsey had a fairly good memory; Filipe had been last assigned to inspect the (hull).

"Filipe?" Kelsey said with no emotion in his voice, sounding little like a question, and he tilted his head for the man to follow him away from the group.

The noise of the laughter quieted to silence, but as Filipe slowly rolled to his feet and met Kelsey a few yards from the group, the volume returned to its normal level.

"Yes, captain," Filipe smiled. Kelsey felt as if it was a mock politeness, but took a silent breath through his nose.

"Your duty was to inspect the hull," Kelsey explained, staring the man straight in the eye, "Or am I wrong?"

"Ye're not wrong, captain," Filipe said, swinging his arms behind his back and holding his wrists, in proper military posture.

"Did you miss the spot with the rot?" Kelsey felt the rise of frustration in his gut and chest, but kept his volume low. Calm.

"Must've not seen it," Filipe had a hard time returning Kelsey's gaze, and was squinting in the sun at the ship. "I apologize, captain."

"Filipe," Kelsey raised an eyebrow, copying the man's pose by holding his own wrist behind his back. "You're informing me that you didn't see the rot for two weeks? It's almost as large as that damn pig, and you're saying you missed it on multiple occasions?"

"Yes, sir," only half of Filipe's smirk dropped, one side of his lips curling toward his ear.

The other men had become quiet, listening to the conversation. Kelsey knew they were curious, concerned, and anxious. While Kelsey wasn't a harsh employer, he still was the one to provide food, shelter, and paying work. They respected their captain. Apparently, Filipe didn't, and even if Kelsey didn't care what people thought of him, it was dangerous for a crewmember not to respect the leader.

"Did you not do your rounds?" Kelsey spoke a little louder, making sure the rest of the crew could hear. "Filipe? Did you not do what I pay you for?"

"I must have not seen the rot," Filipe shrugged, his shoulder shaking as if he was trying not to laugh. "Apologies, captain."

"You must find it humorous," Kelsey stepped toward the campfire, his eyes on the pig, his back to Filipe, "That we are now behind schedule to fix your inept ability to do the simple task of checking the ship's health. If the rot had not been reported in time, we could have been taking on water at sea."

"Glad Jonesy has a good eye, then," Filipe muttered quietly.

The rage hit, the steam rose, and Kelsey felt his blood boiling. "You're not getting pay for a fortnight, to make up for the coin already given to you."

"I need that mon-" Filipe's voice rose, but Kelsey spun around on his heels and charged at the man.

"I need an honest crew!" Kelsey snarled, his vision becoming dark around the corners. "Do you think any captain will let you sit around on your arse and drink the ale, and not earn your coin? I'm not your first employer, so I think you already know how the world works."

Filipe glowered at Kelsey, but kept his mouth shut.

"If you desire a new employer," Kelsey brought his tone back to a calm volume, "You can join the British Navy. If you shirked your duties, they'd flog you."

Filipe eyes widened for a moment, glancing down at Kelsey's empty hands.

"I wouldn't force my men to punish you," Kelsey spat, walking to the fire, "Though you deserve it."

Grabbing a pouch of whiskey, Kelsey walked further up the beach. Tall grass began poking out of the sand, and dunes rolled into green hills. At this vantage point, Kelsey could see the surrounding land and sea.

About two miles down the slope, in the dip of the valley, there was a house. It's roof was burning. Redcoats were running around the building, carrying food, objects, people. Seeing this violence only increased the red simmering in Kelsey's vision, and he turned back to the camp and dropped the whiskey to the sand.

"Men," he said, looking each one in the eyes. "Who's feeling restless?"

Chapter 19 - Isla

"It seems you're on the right path, Casper."

The man hadn't stopped smirking since he woke up that morning, and the positive attitude he had felt private, as if Isla wasn't supposed to see how happy or successful he was. He would be staring off into the distance, all sexy and dark, but then catch her looking at him and his lips would become a straight line. Then, after a second or two, he would grin back at her as if he decided it was okay to be seen in such a good mood.

"I am, I believe," Casper said, leaning up against the doorframe of the sheltered hull. Isla kept her eyes forward as she guided the boat back east, but she could feel the heat of his eyes on her body. She could see his face in her peripheral, and he was either watching the sea out front or staring at the back of her head. "I still need to do some reading later, brush up on my notes and record findings."

"Will you be going to the library?"

"I didn't know there was one," Casper was eating oatmeal out of a bowl, and Isla could hear the clinking of a spoon against glass. "I was planning on going to the coffee shop by Billy Bob's and using my laptop."

"That's a good idea, too," Isla thought about the chain cafe on Main Street, and all the times she went there to study back in high school. "It can get loud, though. Especially when children get out for the day."

"I'll keep that in mind," Casper's footsteps let Isla know he was walking to the stairs, and she peeked over her shoulder to confirm it. Once he was out of sight, she glanced down at the stereo by her feet. All she's wanted to do since yesterday was read the documents, especially the ones written by her father. Not knowing what they said made her anxious, but she didn't want Casper to know what she found. Something instinctual told her it would be a bad idea, as well as the strange note address to her. *Urchin.*

"What are your plans?" Casper's voice came back, along with his footsteps, and he settled back against the doorframe.

"Huh?" Jostled out of her thoughts, Isla turned to see him. His arms were crossed and he was facing the side of the boat, his eyes on the water.

"For the next two days," he said, meeting her eyes, "Do you have any plans?"

"Oh," she nodded, tapping a peg on the hull with her thumb, "I have some personal matters to attend to."

Casper was quiet for a minute, which made Isla start to think about the list of chores she needed to *actually* do when she arrived to shore. Finding the documents had stirred something inside her, like an energy, motivation, to sort through her father's belongings. She needed to start somewhere, and she had a feeling that going through the disastrous attempt at a library would give her answers to whatever was in the ziplock bag. Maybe not. Perhaps the stacks he had were old magazines and newspapers. The dining room table *did* have five stacks of unopened mail advertisements, each ranging from three to five inches high. She should start with the trash, then work her way to the more important papers.

"It seems something's bugging you," Casper said, once again pulling her back to reality, "If you want to talk about it, I'm a really good listener."

"Are you, now?" Isla grinned, scheming a way to change the subject. When she looked back at him, she saw the look on his face; he wanted to hear. Sighing, she pulled up a heavy stool and sat in front of the hull, focusing on the water as she spoke. "I have to clean out my father's house. He died last spring, and I've been putting it off."

"I thought there was an older man who ran this boat," Casper spoke softly. "I saw him in the photo gallery on your website, when I was looking for a charter."

"Yep, that's him," Isla remembered when her father had designed the website, or his attempt to design it. It was a gaudy HTML page from the days of MySpace, and he had rented a book from the library on setting up text boxes and pages. It probably hasn't been updated in almost a decade. "You know, I have a life back on the east coast. Or I did, three months ago. But it's hard to move on from here."

"I understand," Casper said when Isla said no more. "I lost my sister recently, and it's really difficult to get back to a normal life."

Looking at the man, Isla knew they had come to some understanding. They both had felt loss, and it seemed the sadness in Casper's eyes meant he hadn't healed from the trauma yet. Just like Isla.

"I'm sorry," she said, placing her hand on Casper's arm. "You're traveling, at least. Doing what you love. It seems you've been able to pick up the pieces and pressed on."

A series of emotions passed over Casper's pace, first surprised, next was a gentle expression, and finally a bitterness and anger. Isla pulled her hand back and pretended to check the dials near the hull, even though she knew her speed, direction, and acceleration without having to look.

"You're not doing what you love?" Casper asked, his tone sharp, and the air growing tense between them. "Bringing divers out here so they can see the beauty of the sea."

"That's not what I meant," Isla said, shaking her head, "I just meant, it seems you aren't stuck on the death of your sister, seeing as you've traveled across the Atlantic to search for sea slugs. A depressed person would be stuck, frozen in time and place. In a state of shock."

"Not everyone expresses sorrow the same way," Casper stood up from the doorframe, arms still crossed, and he stepped over to the side of the boat.

Unable to step away from the hull, Isla huffed and glanced through the side window to see the American. He was still looking out at the waves, misery shrouding his shoulders and face. It wasn't until now that Isla noticed that his dark demeanor was due to this sadness, this anger held in the forefront of his brain. Sure, he was mysterious, but the darkness was caused by the same reason that Isla's shoulders slumped, why it seemed impossible to smile some days.

At first, she wanted to approach him and apologize. But she turned and stared at the front of the boat, keeping the (front point) lined with her horizon. The coastline was coming into viewing in tiny centimeters, and part of her was ecstatic to get off this boat. She didn't like the way Casper tried pushing her to speak of her feelings. She already hated feeling this way, so why would she want to talk about it?

"Isla," the man came up to the small opening in the side window, apparently no longer interested in talking to the back of her head, "I'm sorry."

"Don't be," she shrugged, not looking at him, "You're right. I shouldn't have made those assumptions."

"Yes," Casper laughed, looking down at his shoes. "I told you I'd listen, so..."

"So?" Isla ran a hand through her hair, giving him a nervous glance. "Your father?"

Sighing, Isla rolled her eyes. "I think I've shared enough, honestly. You're a customer, and I shouldn't have shared personal details with you."

Her interactions with Casper were getting inappropriate, not sexualy but too personal. While there were no rules, or even ethics, against becoming friends with a customer, this excuse was the best way to keep him at arm's length. He was pressing her and she wanted it to stop. Well, a small acorn-sized part of her wanted to keep going, but she didn't want that feeling to grow.

"We will reach the dock in about an hour," she said, nodding to the coastline rising in the distance. "In the meantime, you can finish up the supplies for lunch."

In the corner of her eye, Isla could see Casper's face. He watched her, his expression almost knowing. Knowing her attempts at deflection. His face disappeared, and the sound of his footsteps came from the staircase.

Chapter 20 - Casper

As unsettling it felt to leave Isla and the Eimear with unresolved confusion, Casper felt a weight lift from his chest when he walked along the wooden dock toward the boathouse. He had nodded, said blanket phrases of appreciation, and pushed Logan's cart with all the rental gear away from the boat.

Pushing the cart into the boathouse, Casper almost bumped into Tagh, who had decided to lay in the middle of the floor.

"Excuse me," Casper cleared his throat, hoping the dog would get the message. Nope.

"Tagh, come on," a string of Gaelic words escaped Logan's lips, and the dog huffed in annoyance before standing up to settle under the office desk. "How's the trip?"

"Pretty successful," Casper rested the cart in the corner of the room, and reached for his cellphone. "I'll transport everything once Bill drives up."

"You can leave it here, now," Logan stood up and grabbed a broom from the backroom, and began sweeping dirt in the direction of the open door. "You're only back in, what, three days?"

"Two," Casper grinned, tapping the top of one of the empty oxygen tanks.

"Och, yeah," the older man paused the broom, resting his hands on the top of the handle, "Just leave 'em here. 'Cept the tanks, of course."

"Thank you," Casper said, dialing Billy Bob's Dive Shop. The dive shop owner answered after the third ring.

"Billy Bob's, how can I help ye?"

"Hi, it's Casper Shaw. Is it possible for you to bring seven oxygen tanks to the docks and pick up the empties sometime in the next two nights?"

"Did you just arrive?"

"Yes, but it isn't urgent—"

"I'll be there in a blink!" The line went dead, and Casper sighed, slipping the phone back into his coat pocket.

"He's running over now, ain't he?" Logan asked, sweeping the last bit of dirt out through the front door.

"Bill?" Casper asked, trying to sound distant and uninterested from the local drama. "Yeah. He's very kind."

"He's just trying to bump into Isla, you know."

Unsure how to respond, Casper focused on setting all the rental gear against the corner wall. The empty oxygen tanks were left on the cart, and Casper kept a grip on the cart's handle, itching to leave. Tagh's loud snores rumbled against the floorboards, and Casper could feel the vibrations through his shoes.

Five minutes passed since the phone call, and Bill appeared in the doorframe. He immediately greeted Tagh with a mess of incoherent words that only dog lovers understood, running his hands over the beast's fury head and ears.

"I got you the seven in the back of the truck," Bill stood up and waved at Logan before grabbing the cart's handle. He stood a little too close to Casper, but the American tried not to recoil. "Are these the empties?"

"Yeah," Casper let go of the cart and walked to the front door, "Thanks for the help. We literally just got back."

"How was it?" Bill asked, pulling the cart out through the door and around the corner toward the parking lot. The tone of his voice didn't hide his interest in every detail of the trip.

"It was good," Casper said, thinking maybe he should indulge in his impressions of Isla Muir with her former lover. What would Bill think if he knew Casper found the woman attractive?

"You Americans are so vague!" Bill laughed as they reached the back of the pick up truck. "Did you enjoy the beauty of the firth? Did it aid in your expedition?"

"It was truly gorgeous," Casper answered, his hand brushing over the carefully-wrapped metal piece in the inside coat of his pocket. "I can't wait to see more during the next trip."

"Mhmm," the dark-haired man switched the oxygen tanks out, lifting the filled ones onto the cart and vice versa. Half-way through the process, he paused and raised an eyebrow at his customer. "How was the captain?"

"Isla?" Casper had a hard time seeing her as a captain, even though that was clearly what she was. She was incharge of the boat, and she made all the rules on board. "She was very helpful."

"Did she talk much?" Bill said, cocking his head to the side. "Did she seem happy?"

Oh, no. I shouldn't say anything. "She seemed okay. I don't know her, as this is a business relationship."

"Right, of course," Bill gave a forced laugh and continued swapping out the tanks.

Earlier in the day, Isla had drawn the line. Using an icey tone, she reminded Casper that they should not speak of personal matters. He was her customer, and she was providing a paid service. That is all. Still, the words felt as if the woman had shoved him roughly overboard. In the last few days with her, he had felt they had begun developing a relationship; a grey area that fell after first name bases but right before friends. While Casper's goals were not to 'get to know people', he felt different with Isla. He wanted to talk. He wanted to listen.

"I'll roll this back in," Casper took the cart of filled oxygen tanks and started pushing it toward the ramp leading to the boathouse.

"I got it," Bill closed the hatch to his pick up truck and jogged up alongside Casper. "I can give you a ride home, too, if you need."

"I'll walk, but thank you," Casper let the man take over the cart, but followed him down the ramp. Further down the dock by the boat lanes, Isla's feminine form came into view. It was just her silhouette in the bright sun of the early afternoon, the sunlight bouncing off the surface of the water behind her. She seemed to be bathed in gold and blue light, but the shape of her body was dark from shadows.

Surprisingly, Bill didn't seem to notice. He went straight into the boathouse with the cart instead of stopping on the ramp like Casper expected to. Like Casper was doing, staring. It wasn't until he noticed Isla's pacing slowing that he looked away, and met Bill in the doorway.

"Call if you need anything else," Bill said, glancing at last down the dock. His grin relaxed, his mouth dropping slightly as he seemed to register who was approaching them. Gently pushing Casper aside, he stepped onto the ramp and shoved his hands into his coat pockets. "Hey."

Hey? This was going to get awkward, if it hadn't been before.

The woman froze about seven feet away, and Casper could see her distraught expression on her face. In her arms was the large broken stereo, and her backpack was equipped onto her shoulders and back.

"Hey, Bill," she sounded impatient, a little breathless. Maybe she was nervous, seeing her ex-boyfriend. Her eyes flickered to Casper, and the look on her face showed increased frustration. "You need anything?"

"No, I'm all set," Casper said, staring at the stereo, "Oh, do you want me to stop by tomorrow with the second payment?"

"I'd appreciate that," the woman shifted from one foot to the other, her arms struggling to hold the stereo. She seemed to not want to look at Bill but unable to keep her eyes away from him. "Can I get by?"

"Yes, you may!" Bill's voice was high-pitched, as if he was trying to sound funny but failing. "Let me help you, Isla."

"No, I got it," she said sternly, but Bill stepped up and reached out for the stereo. "Stop, I got it."

"It looks heavy," Bill got too close, encroaching into her personal bubble.

Jerking back, Isla pulled the stereo out of Bill's fingertips. The odd shape and weight of the stereo threw her off balance, and Casper watched as she began falling toward the door frame, in his direction. Instinct kicked in and Casper rushed forward, his hands flinging out in front to grasp her arms. His hands caught both her forearms, preventing her from faceplanting against the wooden doorframe, but the stereo slipped out of her hold. The chunky grey plastic slammed against the dock's floorboards, as well as against the big toe on Casper's right foot. The force of the fall caused the screen of the radio to shatter, and small clear pieces smothered the floorboards as well as Casper's shoes. It hurt, but he kept his eyes on Isla.

Her face was inches away from his own, and her eyes were squeezed shut as if she didn't want to see what her ears heard. The world stopped for a moment as everyone waited for the chaos to cease. Heavy footsteps came up from behind Casper, and Logan glared out from inside the boathouse.

"Get home, *buachaill*!" He shouted at Bill, who's shoulders curved a little as if he was trying to hide in plain sight. "I told you to let her be!"

The dive shop owner turned on his heel and hurried back to the parking lot, his head hanging. Logan stepped close to Casper's elbow, glancing around to see the mess.

"I'll sweep this up, Isla," Logan said, gesturing to the shimmering pieces. "You can throw that in the trash by the lot."

"No."

Casper didn't realize he was still holding onto Isla until she pulled away. She knelt down and picked up the stereo, now *definitely* broken. Standing back up, she appeared to have a better hold on the object.

"I'll take care of it at home," she said, looking down at the worn speakers.

"Do you need any help?" Casper asked, raising his eyebrows. "I don't mind."

"You have work to do, don't you?" She asked, turning toward the parking lot.

"I was just going to do it all tomorrow," Casper said, following her to her parked truck. "I'm too tired to read and take notes."

She didn't respond until they reached her truck, where she shoved the stereo into the bed of the pick up. Then she turned to him and gave a humorless smile. "I'm sorry about that. It's... embarrassing."

"It's alright," Casper shrugged, feeling less awkward with Bill gone. "I won't call him until you're gone next time."

"No, no," Isla shook her head, smirking, "It's alright. We all have businesses to run. It's just the woes of living in your childhood town. Everyone has drama."

"I get it," Casper scratched his head and stepped to the side. "I guess I'll see you tomorrow?"

"Yes," Isla's cheeks grew red, he noticed, and she looked down at her shoes, "In the afternoon."

"Cool," the man laughed for no known reason, and turned away slightly. "Bye."

Isla said nothing as he walked across the parking lot and onto the street. Casper felt his own neck and cheeks burning, and a nervous tickle in his lungs. The last time he felt like this was in college, or maybe even in high school. When he told Isla he was too tired to work on his research that evening, he actually was thinking about how distracted he was by his interactions with her. Instead of looking at notes on tide charts and dredging schedules, he could only think about the discussions he had with Isla, and his mixed feelings toward her.

Chapter 21 - Kelsey

Kelsey hated the British. He hated any military, from any country. He believed the world would be better with more civilians taking law into their own hands, which was what he planned on doing with the men who followed.

All the men, save David, Mariano, and three men who were helping with repairs, trailed behind Kelsey up the dunes to the grassy meadow. They may have followed because they thought they had to, or perhaps they really wanted a hand in saving those in need. Doubtful, as Filipe showed his face last in line. It was too late to save his reputation with the captain, but Kelsey appreciated any help.

There were about five redcoats, all dressed in their shiny maroon and crisp white colors. Their dark trifolds were pointed carefully over their foreheads, no doubt hiding the horns spiking from their skulls. As Kelsey and the crew snuck down the hill, pausing behind rocks, the redcoats didn't seem to notice. They were too busy tossing household valuables into a cart, not caring if glassware broke but simply wanting to take. One of the redcoats was pulling a young woman toward the barn, and another redcoat kept an older couple and a teenage boy on their knees, held at gunpoint. The sharp bayonet pointed inches from the older man's neck.

"Mateo," Kelsey whispered, "You take Jonesy and Ruben to the barn and save the girl. The rest of us, we're going for the others at the front of the house."

Mateo led his two assistance away, making a wide arc of the field. They made it about halfway before one of the redcoats shouted at him.

"Hey, you, stop!"

"Go!" Kelsey whispered, and lunged out from behind a thicket.

The crew of fifteen men charged at the redcoats surrounding the wagon. The soldiers were caught off guard, facing the three men heading toward the barn. Muskets swung through the air, but most of the soldiers looked confused, unsure of where to shoot.

In the front, Kelsey pulled his dagger out of his belt and threw it effortlessly at the redcoat guarding the family. The blade dug into the soldier's chest and he placed his fingers to the trickle of blood, falling backward. The older man jumped to his feet and rushed toward the barn, where Mateo, Jonesy, and Ruben had entered.

The three redcoats around the wagon had been busy loading items into the back, so their muskets were not ready for an ambush. Sam, the crewmember with the thickest biceps and chest, threw his body against one of the redcoats. The soldier's body flew backward and slammed against the side of the cart, and he crumpled to the ground. The last two redcoats began running toward the open field, but the rest of the crewmembers chased them down. None of the redcoats could be allowed to live, as they've seen who the saviors were.

Once the threat of the British was clear, Kelsey ordered the men to begin throwing dirt and water onto the fires scorching the roof of the house. The family would still have to sleep in the barn while doing repairs, but there would still be a house to fix instead of the ashes.

"Thank you, sir," the patriarch of the family wobbled on his knees, and a small trickle of blood streamed down the side of his face. He reached his hands out for Kelsey, who accepted them with his own gloved fingers. "Without you, everything would have been ruined."

"You are very welcome," Kelsey smiled, shaking the man's hand to confirm that their hell was over. "Is there anything else we may assist with?"

"You've done more than enough," the man let go of Kelsey and hugged his teenage son and wife. The young woman rushed out of the barn and joined the group hug. "May I ask, what is your name?"

"I shall give you anything else, save my name," Kelsey nodded at the family and stepped toward his crew. "Let's unload their possessions and put the bodies on the cart."

It didn't take long to place all the family's belongings on the ground, and it took less time and less care to place the bodies onto the wagon.

"Farewell, friends," Kelsey waved at the family before cracking the whip at the horses.

With one wagon and three braw stallions, the crew arrived at the beached Crooked Stock. The men working on the ship repairs were almost done, but they would have to wait until nighttime for the high tide to come back in.

"I see you returned with food," said Mariano, drops of sweat beading on his forehead. He patted one of the horses on the broad neck, and the four-legged beast nickered.

"This should prolong our rations," Kelsey said as Jonesy and Ruben took the horses to a patch of grass for them to graze at. "Though we already have more than enough to reach France. We might be able to sell them, if they make it out of British territory."

"I'd rather eat them," Mariano sharpened a tool against a flat rock, then tucked it into his belt. "Since I'll be some time below, think Durand can roast up the chestnut?"

Kelsey glanced at the horse, it's reddish coat of short fur shining in the afternoon sun. "You're more greedy than the pig we just cooked. Let's wait a few days before we hack away at those three."

As Mariano slunked back to the ship, Kelsey smiled and looked around the camp. He spotted David petting one of the horses, his fingers gentle on the muzzle. The boy gazed up at the beast with such awe and loved, as if it were a large puppy. *Damn, he's getting attached.*

A part of Kelsey wanted to get the cook and ask him to strip, roast, and salt the horse, which would make the carpenter happy. Kelsey did nothing, though, as he knew it would be wrong to strip the gentler parts of life from his son. Who knew how much time David had before he had to jump from boyhood to man.

Chapter 22 - Isla

By the time Isla reached her house, the stress and embarrassment from her interaction with Bill had faded, replaced with the fervor to tear open the plastic bag of papers. When she sat down at the dining room table, though, she carefully opened the zipper opening and pulled the documents out as if they would crumble at the slightest movement.

From what Isla could tell, most of the papers weren't older than a few years. Some of the edges were yellowed or torn, but they looked well preserved and out of direct sunlight. Unsure of where to start, she began reading in order of what was on to pof the pile, starting with the sticky note from her father.

It felt odd reading something from him since he wasn't alive anymore. He must have known she would find these pages, which means he at least suspected something bad would happen that would cause Isla to become the owner of the Eimear. Did he know he was going to die? How does someone know they're going to drown? There were no signs of a struggle, and it was a clear heart attack that caused him to fall overboard. But perhaps something frightened him, causing his heart to stop.

The next page was a letter written by a man named Noah Fallon, and from the contents of the letter, Isla assumed he was a genealogical researcher. The letter was accompanied by the genealogical chart from the *The Genealogy Society of Scotland: Chapter of the West Coast Lowlands and Islands*, the page she had begun reading onboard. Isla's background in genetics was useful in reading the chart, finding the individual in question, then that individuals' parents, grandparents, and further back. The inked names were written small, some of the letters smudged with saltwater, but Isla clearly saw the name: LOGAN WALLACE. Above his name, a line connected two more names: REBECCA WALLACE and LUCAS WALLACE. Using her finger, Isla followed the direct male line, staying with the surname Wallae.

Below each name was a set of years. The birth and death year. The chart had been copied onto a vertically long piece of paper, allowing room to stretch back to the 1700s. The earliest recorded ancestry for Logan was born in 1754 and died in 1819, the name written as David Wallace. It wasn't surprising that there wasn't much information leading back further as many Scottish family records didn't exist or were poorly managed after the Battle of Culloden in 1746. The Jacobites were slashed down in the field, and the British destroyed much of the Scottish culture. Isla's own ancestral history was fuzzy before the 1800's. She only knew that her family had lived in this town since the founding of it, so there hasn't been much confusion there. There was a small plot in the local cemetery that had three decrepit tombstones, all three having the worn engravings with *MUIR* as the last name. These tombstones were set close to the other founding families, so it was assumed that Isla's family had never left the town.

The Muir family would never leave, apparently, as Isla came back.

Setting the genealogical chart to the side, Isla wondered why her father would be interested in Logan's ancestors. The old man had a local lineage just as long as Isla's, and he even *knew* Gaelic, another part of Scottish culture that was lost since the control of the British. Many families felt it important to retain their heritage, and would teach their children both Gaelic and English. The Wallaces were one of those families.

The next page in the pile was a bunch of notes, each one starting with a small round bullet point. As Isla read, she recognized that it was also in her father's handwriting, but there was a strange quickness to the writing, as if he was rushed.

> • *Records at library say young boy was lost at sea, close to shore; boy had a nothing but the clothes on his back; boy was delirious from dehydration, claiming to see demons and treasure*

● *Another record says British officer recognized boy from a previous engagement in Spain, but there was very little information after that*

● *Same record mentions the boy had been found a few days after the attack of a pirate ship by the British, which occurred in the deep waters off the southernmost point of Campbeltown. Cannon blasts could be heard all throughout the night, and bystanders saw tiny bursts of light in the distance*

The notes didn't make sense, and they didn't connect to the genealogical chart. It was as if Isla's father only gave the pieces and expected her to know how they related to each other. Why did this matter, though?

There was one more note, written on the last page as a single bullet:

● *Necklace found in backyard under Mary's rose bushes, real silver, wrapped in old burlap cloth; will give to Logan once lineage is confirmed*

Standing up, Isla walked to the door leading to the backyard. Opening the door, she looked out at the overgrown grassy yard. The jungle was surrounded by a metal fence, and a hill rose up to block the views of the yard from the surrounding roads. Just like on the side of the house, the rose bushes were untamed and reckless, curling and twisting around and through the fence. Isla's mother had planted the first bush right in the middle of the fence, and sure enough, there was a three-foot by five-foot uneven hole in the dirt. The shovel still lay on the ground beside the hole, and a pair of dirty leather gloves sat on top of the long wooden handle.

Isla's first thought was *How could I have not seen this in three months?* Her second thought: *Why didn't my father clean up after himself?* The most important thought: *Where was the necklace?*

Closing the door, Isla walked down the main hallway and to her father's study. She placed her hand on the doorknob and took a deep breath before pushing in.

She had seen the mess before, but now that she was trying to find something, the clutter made her more anxious. She turned the light on, hoping it would shine on the necklace and make her search easier. This obviously wasn't going to be easy.

"Okay," she sighed, going to her father's desk and opening the sliding drawers. More papers stuffed the insides, smooshed with pens, stamps, envelopes, and paperclips. The top of his desk was surprisingly neat, with blank paper and new pens organized on the flat of the wood. On the backside of the desktop was a clean glass and a bottle of whiskey, her father's favorite.

Picking the bottle up, Isla glanced at the label. It was the same bottle she had bought him for his birthday last year. It was half-way empty. She opened the top and placed her nose over the opening, breathing in the rich burn of the alcohol.

"Give me some guidance," she said to herself as she poured a small amount of the reddish-golden liquid in the glass. Taking a sip, she looked around the room once more, strategizing. "It has to be here somewhere. I just need to clean... all this."

She finished her drink, poured herself one more, and grabbed a plastic bag from the kitchen. Back in the study, starting with the pile of papers by the window, Isla read through every single document. Trash went into the plastic bag. Anything useful went on the top of the desk. She didn't know why she was so motivated to find the necklace, but she knew it forced her to face her fear.

Chapter 23 - Casper

Unlike many rentals during Casper's travels, the room he was given had a personal bathroom. This meant he could lay in the bathtub as long as he wanted, which he did the minute he arrived. Locking the door, he dropped all his belongings on the made bed and stripped every article of clothing from his body. Being naked felt like a luxury as he always had something clinging to his skin while on the Eimear. The dirt and saltwater from the previous trip formed a thick crusty layer all over him, and he wanted, *needed*, to get clean.

Turning the hot water faucet on, Casper poured a bubble soap solution into the water porcelain tub. Yes, he liked bubble baths. No matter how professional and proper he acted in public, he required certain pleasures while he was alone. Lemon-scented soaps, fuzzy socks that he didn't want to wear during the trip, and towels with the finest threads. He didn't have the room in his bag to bring his own towels from home, so he had to make do with the laundered white linens at the rental. As the water filled the bath, he ran his hand over the towel on the hook. It was fluffy and clean, and that's what really mattered.

Dipping his toe into the water, Casper felt a rush of goosebumps rise along the skin of his leg, up his butt, and along his back. He placed his hands onto both sides of the bathtub edge and gradually lowered himself into the liquid heat. He felt as if he was wrapped in a blanket, completely sealed away from holes where cold could seap in and find him. The soap lingered against his skin, catching on the fine hairs on his forearms, coating them with white bubbles.

Once he felt satisfied with the water level, Casper turned the faucet off and leaned backwards. His shoulders and back pressed against the cold top part of the tub, but he slid down so his whole body emerged in the water except from the neck up. He couldn't see his body through the bubbles. Closing his eyes, he bent his knees more so his whole head disappeared underneath the surface. Heat pushed against his cheeks and hair, filling his ears. He thought about how different this was from scuba diving out in the cold sea. Here, he could hear nothing except a low hum. There was nothing to worry about in this pocket of warmth.

Pushing his head back above the water, Casper rested his upper body against the back of the tub. The cold porcelain transferred heat, no longer chilly the longer he pressed against it. In the water, he ran his hands over his shoulders, arms, chest, abdomen, thighs. He could feel the grime shedding, and he brought a bath sponge from the side of the tub to help scrub off the layer of dirty salt. The bubbles dispersed with time, and the water was no longer crystal clear. It had a faint tint of brown and grey.

Casper shampooed and conditioned his hair, not taking long in this endeavour. He was finished cleaning, but he wasn't done bathing.

There had been little privacy on the Eimear. No time to pleasure himself if the desire arose. Oh, and it did. Now alone in the bathtub, Casper wrapped his hand around himself and began stroking. Staring at the murky image through the water's surface, his eyes glazed over as he thought about Isla.

There was no one else to fill his fantasies. None of his ex-girlfriends came to mind, and no movie stars or hot celebrities. He could only think about the young boat captain, her dark hair tied into a loose braid, strands escaping and blowing in the sharp wind. Her clothing seemed slightly baggy, not form fitting, but her shape could still be made out. The way her hips swayed a little when she rushed across the deck, grabbing equipment and moving things about. The focus in her eyes, the confident and intense air about her.

Her lips, wrapping around a spoon. Her eyes staring back at him.

The release only relaxed Casper even more, but he needed to get out of the tub, more dirty from his efforts. He popped the plug from the drain and climbed out, grabbing the towel on the side. Wrapping the large cloth around his waist, he wiped steam from the mirror. His reflection stared back, and he noticed the bags under his eyes. He would need sleep, but first, he needed to review his notes.

His skin was still damp, so he kept the towel around him as he used dry hands to take out the notebook. He also brought out the silver locket and set it on the wooden surface of the desk, and tried opening it. There was a worn clasp on the side, making it difficult to pry. After three careful but firm attempts, Casper was able to crack the two metal pieces apart. Inside, each metal component had a hollowed out curve. One curve was empty; one had a faded picture that resembled a face.

Flipping through his notes, Casper tried to find the initials K. V. There were no names relating to the letters, historical or contemporary. He didn't know if the locket happened to be an unrelated find, but he doubted that. It related, but he didn't know how yet. Another question he had was how long the locket had been submerged in the saltwater. It had definitely not been three centuries. It looked like a few months, maybe a year or two. So how could his sister have known about a treasure that was "buried" recently? From what Casper knew, Bella hadn't traveled to Scotland in years. She had been focused on a treasure in Central America, not here. But she clearly knew where to search here. She must have had a partner.

Well, she did. Casper was pretty sure her partner was Liam Martinez. Bella and Liam had worked together in two previous explorations before the most recent one, and Casper met the guy once and immediately didn't like him. He was pompous and had a deceptive edge to him, like something just wasn't right about him. But Bella liked working with him, and continued to do so until she was murdered.

Casper believed Liam was the one who killed her.

While there is no proof that Liam *did* kill her, he is the only one with true motive. Bella must have been keeping something from him, her research notes possibly, and he tried getting her out of his way. This might be only Casper's thoughts, but it was his *only* thoughts, and they were getting him through the pain.

Isla had been wrong about pain and depression. She had said someone who was stock, unmoving, was the one unable to move on. Well, Casper couldn't *stop* moving. If he did, the anger of his sister's death and the pain of her loss would rush into his chest, and he wouldn't be able to move again. He knew he would have to pause eventually, but not now. He was so close to finding what Bella was looking for, and for the reason she was murdered.

Chapter 24 - Kelsey

Once the Crooked Stock was patched and fixed, the horses were loaded and the bodies of the British soldiers were buried. In the dark looming night, with a chill in the wind colder than what's found in the brisk Highlands, the crew heaved the ship out, guided by the high tide. Those who preferred working with bare feet felt seashells cut into their skin, and the lick of sand and salt between their numb toes. Nevertheless, Kelsey and his men made their way into deeper waters and away from the beach.

The course would lead them further south as that was the only path to go. North would lead them to colder waters, and Kelsey craved a warmer swim. While the seas brushing against the French coastline were still chilly, compared to the North Sea, they were like a hot bath. What Kelsey would enjoy even more would be to take David on a trip further south, around Portugal, and to the Mediterranean.

Back on board, the crew resumed their assigned shifts. A third of the men went down below to sleep, and the others worked the remainder of the night. Kelsey sent David to sleep as the boy didn't really have a position yet. Some of the crew didn't agree with the way the boy was treated, believing if a boy should live on a ship, he should be treated like all the other sailors. That's how the men grew up, many working at David's age, some younger.

The thing was that David was the captain's son. While nepotism was frond upon, the captain could do what he wanted when it came to certain personal matters. He could stay in his quarters all day, not helping lift sails or carry equipment. He could allow his son to eat extra rations and play tricks on the men. But no, his son did his share of work, though it may be light.

For David, Kelsey had a different idea of duties. The boy was required to read five pages of a book, or two pages of a newspaper. The only thing was that David already finished all the books on the

Crooked Stock, but still, Kelsey said he had to complete the daily five page work, even if it meant re-reading.

The second duty for David was to write one page in his journal. It could be about anything, but it had to make sense. Recently, Kelsey has been bringing up the idea of supporting arguments, which he thought would be easy for the eight-year-old. The child would write one page extra just to explain why his theory was correct. Perhaps David thought if he did more work one day, he wouldn't have to do it the following day. *No, no, no,* Kelsey would say, *though I like the way you think, you still got your duties to attend to in the morning.*

The third duty for David was to count the coins in Kelsey's desk. There were multiple variations, with currencies from Scotland, England, France, and Spain. David had to write a list of the type of coin, how many coins, and what it amounted to. Every day, Kelsey would add or subtract a few coins from each pile, or sometimes throw in a new foriegn coin. He knew the boy would find it tedious, but David never complained as he jotted the names down and furrowed the piles.

Once the boy had completed his "schooling," he would assist the sailors in any work that required a small-bodied, quick-footed individual. He would wash the deck, tie ropes, climb ropes, run messenger, etc. Despite his morning lessons, his daily life was never the same. Some days he spent helping the cook; other days he was sitting at the top mast with a spyglass, searching for land. Kelsey didn't know a better way to raise a child, or at least refused to see any other way.

In his quarters, Kelsey sorted through his records for reminders. There was a list of items he had to attend to once the sun rose, but for now, he just wanted to sit at his desk and breath. On the other side of the room, David snored softly in his bed. Grinning, Kelsey took a sip of whiskey and stared at his knuckles.

The skin was scraped, with the olive skin pushed back and pink showing underneath. He must have grazed his hand during the departure and not have noticed until now. Pouring a little whiskey on the cuts, he gritted his teeth so as to not wake David. Then Kelsey grabbed a white cloth and wrapped it around his knuckles. Another lesson to teach David: preventing infection.

The crew trusted Kelsey, but they still were wary of his extra care on cleaning wounds. He had known a good physician back in Spain, who taught him to always clean a wound with alcohol so it wouldn't turn green and maggots wouldn't grow. While he never experienced maggot-infected gashes, he rarely had infection ever since he applied the painful stinging liquid.

As Kelsey tucked the ends of the cloth in, he heard a rumbling of footsteps above. He froze in his seat to listen, and recognized the sound as a brawl. So he grabbed his pistol, slid it into his belt, and went up to the main deck.

Most of the working crew were still at their posts, but near the middle of the boat were four crewmembers. They were surrounding a tall, lanky figure who was standing with his back a little too straight. Kelsey approached, silently persuading the crew member to step to the side.

"Who do we have here?" Kelsey asked, his hand on his belt, fingers close to his pistol but still relaxed. "A stowaway?"

The young man met Kelsey's gaze, and Kelsey recognized him. It was the teenage boy from the Scottish farm, the one the crew saved from the soldiers. Immediately, Kelsey let out an annoyed sigh and rolled his eyes.

"Don't tell me you've gone running from your kin," Kelsey said, stepping a little closer so the boy could see the kindness in his eyes.

"I have," the boy said, his chin pointed high in the air. "You can't send me back."

"Well," Kelsey squinted off at the coastline, which was barely visible in the dark night, "I *could*, but you'd find some other way to get yourself in trouble."

"I want to be a sailor," the boy said, his fists clenched in determination. "I want to be like the men on your crew."

Kelsey glanced at the four crewmembers, and at the same time, all five seamen began laughing.

"I'm sorry, I don't mean to insult," Kelsey said when the boy's eyes filled with anger. "I'm honored, and as you can see, I have nothing against my profession, but... sailors aren't the most heroic employments."

"You saved my family," the boy said, gesturing to the hidden coast with his hand. "You all are heroes, and I am in your debt."

Agitation tickled Kelsey's chest, and he stepped closer to the boy. "First lesson of being a sailor, or any man for that matter: Do not seek out a debt. Second lesson: Do not seek payment for righteous deeds."

It was difficult to see in the dim light of the lanterns, but red creeped across the boy's neck and face.

"You're a farmer," Kelsey pinched the boy's arms, examining his build. "You understand physical labor, though that doesn't mean you won't complain. You get a cot down below, food, as well. Pay in two weeks, but only if you complete your duties properly."

The boy's eyes lit up, realizing he wasn't going to get thrown overboard.

"Did you tell your mother your plans?" Kelsey asked.

"I told my parents," the boy glanced at his feet, "Though they wished for me not to go."

"They're house is in need of repairs," Kelsey shrugged, speaking in a matter-of-fact tone. "They needed you to fix their roof, and now you're gone."

"I'll send money to them," the boy's eyebrows pinched together. "I'll write to them once we reach land."

"We've all said that," Sam said, leaning against a stack of boxes near the stairs. "Only some of us keep our word."

"Sam," Kelsey held his hand out for the boy to meet the burly sailor, "May you give our new crewmember an introduction. What's your name, boy?"

"Ryan MacLean," the boy's eyes glued to Sam's massive pectoral muscles, which were less intimidating in the low light.

"Ryan, welcome to the Crooked Stock," Kelsey grinned, "I'm Captain Kelsey Vargas, and our next destination *est le littoral français*."

Chapter 25 - Isla

The next day, there were two black trash bags waiting for trash day by the front door, and Isla had only finished cleaning her father's study after lunch. Many of the papers were copies, scans of book pages. It appeared there were three stacks of books and papers, organized by her father. One pile was useless records and didn't relate to his unidentified search; one pile, the smallest one, had information that pertained to the search; the last pile was a mismatch of sources, so seemed to be the stack her father hadn't gone through yet.

Isla went through the unread stack, skimming through the table of contents and indices for anything that stuck out to her. Local history, references of the late 1700s, etc. There were only three sources that felt useful, so the rest went to the large pile of junk. She placed all the junk items against the wall by the window, but organized it so the light came through from outside. Turning around, she couldn't help but smile.

Previously cluttered, the room was no longer an eyesore. The red Persian rug could be seen, as well as the hardwood floor on the edges of the floor. The "keep" pile fit perfectly next to the desk, reaching almost the top of it. Later, Isla would donate or sell the books, but not right now. This was a time to clean.

Well, it was now time to rest. Dust and sweat clung to Isla's clothes and skin, and she needed to take a break from all the reading and thinking she did while cleaning. She still smelled of the sea, as well as three days of not bathing, so she went upstairs. After a mindless, quick shower, she pulled on an oversized sweater and black leggings, and went back down to the study. She just wanted to see the progress and it made her feel giddy and weightless.

Her stomach growled, so she stepped out of the room and closed the door. When she walked into the kitchen, the happy feelings in her chest deflated. There was so much more cleaning to be done in here, and in the living room, and all the rooms upstairs. Not to mention the closet.

It had taken her hours to go through her father's study. How long would it take to finish the rest of the house? She was exhausted, her brain was foggy, and her back muscles ached. The shower had been helpful but didn't give her the relaxation she had sought.

The first thing she needed to do was take care of the stereo. When she had arrived home, she had set it down on the dining room table and forgotten about it. Now, she pushed it against the wall, wondering how bad it would be to leave it there as a decoration piece. The front display was smashed from the fall. It couldn't be used as a radio, and it was manufactured right before CDs became popular.

It played music by tape. Opening the cassette player, Isla saw the rectangular object. It was the size of her hand, and had a string of black tape looped inside it. She remembered her mother donating a whole box of cassette tapes back in the early 2000's, but this one must have been forgotten. Ejecting the tape, Isla held it up to read the label. It was blank.

Usually there would be a playlist name written in sharpie, or some theme or indication of what was on the tape. This cassette tape was labeled "The Proclaimers", with the years 1994 written below it.

Inserting the tape back into the player, Isla tried turning the stereo back on. The radio had broken, and many of the outside was cracked, but sometimes old objects worked better than their modern descendants. Isla remembered blowing on floppy disks to make them work, or banging on the side of an old grey box with an outdated manufacturer's logo. Technology didn't work like that now.

Isla's hope turned into disappointment as the stereo powered on but didn't turn the wheels of the cassette tape. Powering the machine back off, she pulled the cassette tape back out and slid it into a plastic bag. She would store it with her father's more precious belongings, when she came to sorting them.

As Isla reached for the refrigerator door, she heard a knock on the front. Her hand paused as she thought about who could it be. No one ever visited, though everyone in town said they wound. She was glad they didn't keep their promises.

"Isla?"

Casper! He said he would drop the check off in the afternoon. Glad she had spruced herself up, Isla hurried to the front door and opened it halfway.

"Hi," she said, peering up at the blonde handsome man. "How was your night?"

"Great, relaxing," he smiled at her, and she felt her heart pump a little faster. "I came by to drop this off."

Isla saw the envelope in his hand, and she nodded and reached out. "Thanks."

Hesitant, he handed it to her. He looked behind her, appearing interested in seeing where she lived. Who she was.

"Want to come in?" she heard herself saying without really thinking it first. The words tumbled out and lay exposed in the air between her and Casper.

"Sure."

Isla closed the door behind him and led him down the hallway to the kitchen. She immediately regretted inviting him inside when she saw the mess of papers.

"I'm still organizing my father's belongings," she said, wondering if Casper cared at all. "Sorry about the mess."

"It's alright," he said, his American accent making his 'r' fixed and enunciated. "There's so many papers."

"I know," she laughed, placing the envelope of cash on the table and stepping toward the fridge. "Are you hungry?"

"I didn't eat lunch yet, so yeah," he met her gaze. "I was thinking we could go out for lunch. I've only eaten the rental owner's meals, and they are delicious, but I want to try some of the restaurants."

"You're staying with Mary, right?" She thought about the little old woman, plump and running her own bed and breakfast. She had been a distant friend of Isla's mother, way back when.

"Uh huh," Casper stuck his hands in his pockets and tilted his head to the side, "So what do you say?"

"To what?" Isla's brain was still misty from the work of the day, and her wit wasn't quick like usual.

"Eating lunch with me?"

"Oh, yes!" Isla exclaimed, then her face turned red as she realized she sounded too excited. "Yes. Give me a few minutes to get ready. I need to get out of here."

"It's good to take a break from all this," Casper's voice followed her down the hallway as she grabbed her coat and looked for her wallet. "How long have you been working on this?"

"All night," she said, searching for her black leather wallet that usually rested on the hallway table. "Do you see a black wallet in the kitchen?"

There was a moment of silence before Casper responded. "Yeah, here it is."

"Oh, I'm so out of it," Isla said as he came down the hallway, holding out her wallet.

"Did you say all night?" Casper asked as they walked outside. "Did you sleep at all yesterday?"

"I forgot," she shrugged, locking the front door. "I started working on something and lost track of time. Then sometime between two o'clock and three, I must have fallen asleep on the floor. I woke up at five and couldn't go to bed once I was up."

"Do you usually stay up late?" It sounded as if Casper was genuinely concerned, but Isla didn't know if he was just making small talk.

"No," she unlocked her car and they slid into the front seats, "Not usually."

"Would you rather stay and go to bed early?"

"I can't be in that house for a few hours," Isla backed the truck up onto the street and headed into town. "I'm counting on you to distract me, Casper."

A deep-chested laugh came from the man's throat. "I'm sure I'll find a way."

Chapter 26 - Casper

The drive into town was a short one, but Casper felt like it wasn't going to end. Though he acted confident and relaxed around Isla, his heart raced and his palms were sweaty. She acted like he felt, speaking in random bursts about various topics, like the weather which never changed. She pointed out a few individuals who lived in town, but never indulged in gossip or grudges. She may have hated the townsfolk but she never let on. They were pieces in this world that moved about, just as she did, with their own lives and loves and problems.

There was a little restaurant on the same street as the bank and Billy Bob's Dive Shop, but it was far down so Casper couldn't see the red and white sign. It was for the best that they didn't bump into Bill as Casper regretted bringing him to the dock the previous day. Isla did not want anything to do with the former lover, that was for sure. Casper didn't know if it was because of Bill's annoying and overly-generous personality, or if Bill acted that way because of the break up. Either way, Casper felt bad about pulling Isla into the situation, and didn't want it happening again.

Also, he wanted time with her.

Having a brief fling with Isla Muir had crossed Casper's mind countless times since they left the Eimear, and the more he thought about it, well, the more he thought about it. She seemed somewhat interested in his company, especially with her jokes and interest in his life. While he didn't want to reveal his secrets, he enjoyed having someone notice him.

"They have really good haggis in here," Isla said as they climbed out of the parked truck and walked to the entrance of the restaurant. "They make it a little different than other places do."

"I bet each family has their own secret recipe," Casper said, holding the door open for her to walk through, "Carried down through generations."

"It's usually the same recipe," Isla laughed, pausing at the check-in booth, "But not here."

The hostess seated them at a table on the side wall, toward the front window. Casper sat with his back to the glass window, more comfortable seeing the whole room in front of him.

"I heard haggis can make you sick," he whispered to Isla after the hostess left.

"If not prepared correctly," Isla said, nodding, "But so are mussels and clams, and chicken. Even beans."

"Beans?" Casper grinned, furrowing his eyebrows. "How so?"

"Did you know that raw kidney beans are poisonous?" Isla asked rhetorically, grabbing a napkin and placing it on her lap. "Then there's the purple taro root that if eaten raw can kill you. But it's used a lot in ice cream and other Asian recipes."

"I didn't know they had taro root ice cream here?" Casper said, wondering how Scottish-made Asian recipes would taste.

"They don't," Isla's smile faded a little, her eyes becoming distant. "You must realize just because this is a small country town, the people here are educated and have experienced the world. Most of us aren't as—"

"I didn't mean offense," Casper interrupted, his cheeks warming, but Isla held her hand up in the air and cut him off.

"Do not interrupt me," she said, her tone firm but not loud.

Mouth shut, the man felt his whole face go red.

"Scottish people aren't ignorant," she continued, "And I'd like to try and think Americans aren't, either. No matter how the media portrays you all."

She had finished speaking right when the waiter came over with his little notepad and pen.

"What can I get you all this afternoon?"

"I'll have the All-American burger," Isla said, her eyes not looking at the menu but directly at Casper's face, "A classic BLT."

"Sure thing," the waiter said, writing it down, "And to drink?"

"Scotch," she said, glancing over at the bar, empty of customers. "Please."

"And for you, sir?"

Skimming through the menu, Casper sighed and pointed at a selection. "Haggis, with the vegetables. And could I have a beer?"

"What type?"

"Uh..." shrugging, Casper glanced at the bar, "Tennent's, please."

"Okay," the waiter said, taking the menus, "I'll get your drinks and place your order with the cook."

As the waiter walked away, Casper realized there was no one else in the restaurant to eat. It was only around three thirty, so not many people wanted to dine out yet.

"I feel like I keep saying the wrong thing," he told Isla, breaking the uneasy silence, "With you. And I don't want to offend you anymore."

She said nothing as her eyes settled on his hands, which were fiddling with the napkin on the top of the table. "I guess that's an apology."

"But you also do the same," he hurried to say, his whole body feeling as if it was on fire, and he wanted to run away. "Like bringing up grief."

"We're still getting to know each other, Casper," Isla said, tilting her head to the side a little, "And there is a small cultural difference."

"Yeah," he leaned back in his chair, nodding, "I'm sorry. This doesn't really matter, anyways. I don't know why I brought it up."

The waiter delivered their drinks and left. Isla picked up her Scotch and took two long sips before setting the glass back down on the table. She looked as if she was preparing to say something, and needed the liquid courage to help her.

"I've been living at my dad's house," she said, her eyes focused on her glass, "For three months, since he died. I haven't touched a goddamn thing until last night when I cleaned his study. And I feel elated but also... I'm not sure how to describe it."

Wanting to say something, Casper kept his lips together. He needed to listen, no matter what he thought should be said.

"I'm about to lose my research position at the university," Isla continued, then finished her glass before speaking again, "Because I've pretty much abandoned them. I would never have thought I would just leave my friends and colleagues, but it was so easy. So fluid to just disappear in this town. But I can't disappear here when everyone knows me. Everyone loved my dad."

The waiter came over and, after Isla's request, came back with another glass of whiskey.

"I broke up with Bill before I moved away," Isla said, glancing at Casper's eyes before quickly looking away, "He wanted to get married and start a family. I wanted to get out of here, not be stuck here. So I left, buried myself in my research. I love what I do, but I know that can't be all. When I came back here, Bill thought it was a sign from God that we were meant to be together. He probably still does, and I just want to figure out how to move on."

"I'm sorry about yesterday," Casper said, the urge to say it exploding inside him. "If I had known how pushy he'd be, I would have waited."

"It's not your fault," Isla swirled the liquid in the bottom of the glass, "You don't control how he acts; only he does that."

"Do you love him?" The question came out of nowhere, but now it was out in the open.

Isla looked surprised, her eyes meeting Casper's before shaking her head a little. "No. I don't think I ever did. I was comfortable with him, and we were friends, but there was no passion. I didn't care about his goals or ambitions, like partners should. At least, I think that's how a relationship should be."

"Challenging?" Casper grinned.

"Kind of, yes," Isla chuckled, "Where the two people challenge each other to be better versions of themselves. But the relationship shouldn't be hard, or a struggle. If that makes sense."

"It does," Casper took a large gulp of his beer, his nerves settling.

The waiter brought the meals out, and Casper's stomach churned from being empty. Both Isla and Casper gave the waiter quiet "thank you"s and head nods before furiously digging into their food.

"This is pretty tasty," Casper said, mulling the diced meat and vegetables around his mouth. "How d'you like the burger?"

"I love burgers," she said, biting a huge chunk from the side of hers. "I prefer more spicy options, but these are good."

"Have you been to the United States?" Casper asked.

"No," she spoke with her mouth full, hiding her moving lips with her hand, "I've visited Europe, did some work in the Mediterranean, as well as Mozambique. I've thought about visiting a friend in Canada, but I've never had the time."

"Mozambique?" He asked, thinking of where that was. "Oh, on the east coast of Africa?"

"Yes," Isla gave him an odd expression, her eyes fixated on his face for a moment. "It's like one of the top research spots for marine biologists. Especially for nudibranchs."

Something caught in Casper's throat, and it wasn't food or beer. He felt a chill run up his spine, and he looked away from Isla's gaze. He should be more careful about what he knows and doesn't know, or she'll find out how little he knows.

Chapter 27 - Casper

Casper had thought Isla had a high tolerance for alcohol, but even the Scottish captain had her limits. She had two quick shots of whiskey early in the meal, and had a large glass of wine while eating her cheeseburger and fries. While the fatty substance helped in slowing her inebriation, once she had finished her plate, she requested the waiter for another glass of wine.

"There's this thing that my father has been working on," she said, her voice louder than normal, her words a little slurred. "This project, I guess. He was obsessed with it, searching for something."

"What do you mean?" Casper had the familiar intrigue of a search, but really was interested in listening to Isla's slow unravel into drunkenness.

"He has all these papers around the house," Isla smiled at the waiter as he set down another large glass of red wine, "About the history of the town. The ancestry of certain people. None of it is connected though! I don't know how it all goes together."

"Did your father work for the heritage society?" Casper asked, taking a sip of water. "Or the library?"

"No," Isla paused for two seconds to drink her wine. "He was pure sailor. At least, I thought he was. Most of the papers were from regional organizations, but a few were from the library. There's no notebook or list explaining their purpose."

Thinking of Bella's notebook, Casper set down his glass of water and took a deep breath through his nose. A local boat captain doing research? What kind of research?

"What are the details of these documents?" He asked, attempting to sound vaguely curious.

"Och, mostly ancestry," Isla's eyes tracked people and cars that traveled by the window front behind Casper. "My father was looking into Logan's, though there was no note saying why. I assume that Logan asked my father to do some digging, but I don't want to bring it up to him in case he hadn't."

"Why would your father be looking at Logan's ancestors?" Casper leaned forward, resting his elbows on the white table cloth.

"Perhaps there was some question to his Scottish lineage," the woman shrugged one shoulder, "Though I thought his family was almost as old as mine. Settling here a little after my ancestors helped start the town."

"It is strange," Casper ran a finger over the bridge of his nose and glanced at his watch. "It is getting late, and I would like to rest for tomorrow."

"It's really nice to see a dedicated researcher," Isla said suddenly, reaching her hand across the table and resting it on Casper's wrist. "Official or not."

Like earlier, Casper's blood turned cold.

"My father seemed to be a citizen investigator," she continued, looking down at the dirty napkin she had placed on the table, "Though I wish I had gotten to speak with him about it. And you, Casper, you are so focused on finding your little white sea monsters."

Isla's words were very slurred, her speech somewhat incoherent.

"I'm almost inspired to return to my own work," her face dropped, and tears formed in her eyes.

"Let's get you home, Isla," Casper raised his hand and the waiter came over. "We're ready for the check, please."

"Certainly," the waiter took no note of the change of mood as he left.

"If I had only listened to him," Isla was saying quietly, her face turned down, "Maybe he'd still be alive. I may have been able to save him."

"Hey," Casper took her hand that was on his wrist, and held it gently in both of his hands. Her fingers were cold. "I'm going to drive your truck back to your home. Is that alright?"

Nodding, she closed her lips, not meeting his eyes. The waiter returned and placed the bill on the table. Casper used his free hand to quickly drop a set of bills under the bill and stood.

"Come on," he spoke softly to Isla, who appeared ready to break down any second.

After taking her keys out of her coat pocket, he helped slip her coat onto her arms but didn't bother zipping it up. She wasn't stumbling but was not as coordinated as her sober self, so he wrapped his arm around her back and led her to the truck.

As Casper helped her into the passenger seat, Isla mumbled something.

"What?" he asked, leaning his head closer to hear her.

"I don't know where the necklace is."

Casper looked down at the paved parking spot for any jewelry. "Did you lose it?"

"I can't find it," she whispered, her eyes closed, her hands still on her lap. "I don't know where he left it."

Confused, Casper closed the car door carefully as not to hit the woman. "Want me to look inside for it?"

Isla shook her head a little. Sighing, Casper climbed into the driver's seat and started the truck. He pointed the heater toward Isla, hoping her hands were normally cold to the touch. He also hoped the short drive to her house would sober her up, but it only seemed to change her mood.

The sun had finished setting as Casper parked in her driveway. He turned the truck off and went around to the other side to open her door. She opened her eyes and stuck her foot out, an apparent attempt to step out of the seat. She didn't have control over her legs, so she began falling toward the ground.

"Whoa," prepared for something like this, Casper's arms were already out to catch her. "You feeling okay?"

"Too much," she said, her fingers gripping the front of his coat. "I'm sorry."

"It's okay," like at the restaurant, he held one arm around her waist. His other hand held her arm. "Let's get you to the door."

Once they were at the door, he fumbled through her keys, searching for the one for the house. Isla pointed to one covered in green tape, so he used it to unlock the front door.

"Here's your keys," he placed the keys in her hand and closed her fingers around it. "I'll leave you here. Go get some water and get changed."

Isla's gaze was on his face, looking unsteady with a strange dreamy expression. When Casper finished speaking, she stepped forward and stood on the balls of her feet. Her lips pressed against his, and he froze on his stance on the doormat.

Her lips were soft, warm, unlike her hands. She wasn't trying to pry his mouth open or rip into his face with her tongue. It was a sweet, delicate movement. Still, Casper felt wrong since she was drunk and he was not.

He placed his hands on her upper arms and drew her back down to her heels. She looked very confused and disappointed, and despite his decision, so Casper felt the same way.

"Come inside," she said, partially sounding like a question. Partially like an order.

"No," he responded firmly, letting go of her arms and stepping to the side. "I'll wait until you go in and lock the door. I want to make sure you are safe before I leave."

For all he knew, she could choke on her own vomit after he left. But he didn't want her to do anything more foolish or dangerous. His feelings didn't show on his face, but he wanted to kiss her back. He wanted to take her inside, through the hallway, to the kitchen, and do more than kissing on her kitchen table. But no. She wasn't in the right state of mind, even if she hadn't a lick of wine or whiskey.

"Understand?" Casper asked as she stared up at him.

Nodding, Isla stepped through the threshold and slowly closed the door. Casper placed his hand on the door to pause her for a moment.

"I'll see you tomorrow," he said, smiling at her.

Not returning his smile, she closed the door. A subtle click affirmed that the lock was in place, and Casper felt confident to leave. He walked to the end of the walkway and turned to look at the house. There weren't any windows he could see through, or none that had lights to show the inside of the rooms. Though the house was dark, he could feel the sad Scottish woman staring out at him. When he walked out of view of the house, the feeling disappeared.

Chapter 28 - Isla

Hangovers were not new to Isla, but she hadn't experienced one in almost a decade. At least not since finishing her post baccalaureate degree. She woke up in her bed, still dressed in the jeans and shirt she wore last night. The room spinned a little, but she was more focused on the pounding ache on the right side of her head, right above her eye. Sweat stuck her clothes to her skin and she felt a little nauseous.

She wasn't able to wake up on her own. A buzzing from the sheets roused her consciousness, and she opened her eyes. The curtains were pulled shut over the window, but a small vertical line of sunlight landed right on her face. She groaned and reached for the cellphone, which had been left, uncharged, under a pile of sheets.

Just the alarm. Thank god, she didn't sleep through it. Still, her body felt as if she had slept through the whole morning.

There was a large bottle of water on the nightstand, and she vaguely remembered putting it there before passing out on the mattress last night. She took the water and chugged half of it, then let out a large burp that rumbled through her stomach and esophagus. Her skin felt flaky and dry, and her hair had knots.

She had an hour to get ready, which usually was enough time for her in the mornings. This morning, she moved slowly. After ten minutes of sitting cross-legged in bed and staring at the crumpled blankets and sheets, she rolled herself to the edge and stood to her feet. There was a small sensation of vertigo, but she made her way to the bathroom. It took her twice as long to accomplish a semblance of good hygiene and pack a bag. She didn't need to bring much as she still had extra clothes and supplies on the Eimear, but she did want to bring an extra heavy coat. A cold front was expected to blow in during the night, and she didn't want to be freezing while trying to sleep down in the cabin.

Down in the kitchen, Isla made an attempt to eat breakfast. She nibbled at a few flakes of cereal, drank a tablespoon of milk, before cleaning up her meal. She would eat later once her stomach no longer felt queasy. Thinking of nothing else she could do at the house, she picked up her bag, locked the front door, and drove to the docks.

There were a few memories poking in through the fog from last night. Isla remembered finishing her meal. She remembered Casper driving her home. She also remembered the embarrassing fumble of her lips attacking his face. Oh, how could she face him now? Live with him for the next three days in a tiny vessel on the sea? She was surprised she didn't receive an email or text from him, canceling the whole trip. From what she could remember, he didn't seem upset last night by anything she had said or did. His calm composure didn't mean anything, though, as he could have been being polite. Understanding.

A tiny sliver of worry lingered inside Isla's chest. *What did I tell him? Did I tell him about Dad's research?*

Unlike the last few times, Isla wasn't the first to arrive at the Eimear. The tall blonde American was sitting on a wooden post, flipping through his tattered notebook, Logan's cart ready to be unloaded of the dive equipment. When Isla walked up, Casper closed his notebook and gave a weak smile.

"Hey," he greeted, and there was a gentle but humorous note to his voice.

Fuck, this is going to be painfully awkard. Isla nodded at him. "Casper."

"How are you feeling?" he asked, stepping away from the post and storing his notebook in his backpack.

"I'm fine," she shrugged, and hopped onto the boat. "Let's get going."

As they loaded the boat and strapped equipment and tools down, Isla wondered how sluggish she looked. Did Casper notice? Of course he noticed as she had a feeling he noticed everything. It took a little longer to get everything sorted on the main deck, and Isla's decision making was slightly delayed. The brain fog was clearing from when she woke up but was still there in the front of her mind. She wore a old blue cap, which shielded the glare of the sun through the thick white clouds, but she didn't have any sunglasses.

"Here's the locations," Casper handed her the list of GPS coordinates, and she recognized the first one. "I've decided to go back to this one before we travel further out."

Isla took the piece of paper and taped it to the little window behind the helm. She checked all the switches and monitors, like doing a quick check of a car's dashboard or an airplane's control system. Everything was in working condition.

"Do you feel okay to drive?" Casper asked from the helm's doorway.

Isla felt heat spread through her body and she whipped around to look at him. "I'm not drunk anymore. I'm just hungover."

She didn't mean for her words to come out so rough, but control was difficult for her at the moment. Casper did a tight lipped grimace, nodded, and went downstairs to the deck below. Isla started the boat and directed it out into the brightening sea. As she stood at the helm, she reached down to flick the radio on. Her hand connected with empty air, and she looked down. Right. There was nothing to listen to except her thoughts, the last thing she wanted.

Chapter 29 - Casper

Casper stayed below deck until he felt the boat's speed slowing. Isla needed to be alone and he wasn't going to pester her with his presence. If he had a massive hangover with awful, embarrassing memories, he would want to be left to sort his feelings out.

The ride out to the firth was quiet as there was no music blasting from the stereo. There was the emergency radio, used to communicate with Logan on land and other emergency personnel if need be. The lack of old classic rock made the boat feel bare, and Casper had nothing to listen to except his thoughts and the creaks of the boat. He really didn't need to study his notebook so he took one of the ten books from the small shelf by the eating area.

They were all ratty paperbacks, the flimsy covers torn around the edges. Two were historical fishing guides, but the others were stereotypical romances. A man looking like Fabio posed on the front cover, and in his muscular, protective arms was a woman who appeared to be in a trance at the sight of him. The wear on the pages suggested they had been read multiple times, and the same messy name was signed on the first page of each novel: Onora Ruthven.

It must be Isla's mother's collection.

Choosing the book about a swashbuckling pirate, Casper laid in his small bed and read the first few chapters. The details were exaggerated and the sex was overhwleming, but it was something to focus on instead of the silence. When he was reading the ending of the first steamy scene, he felt the boat slow and a shout from above. Setting the book on his blanket, Casper grabbed his clothes and changed into a warmer set of fleece. Then he went up to the main deck and found Isla lowering the anchor.

"The waves aren't as choppy as the first time around," Isla said, sounding less irritated than before. "You should have a smoother dive today."

He said nothing as he climbed into the dive suit. When he needed help with the zipper, Isla quietly came up to his side and pulled the suit shut. He felt awkward, waiting for her to make a joke or say something with her light attitude. But her face was blank except for a tension in her eyebrows.

"Thank you," Casper said, trying to mentally make her look him in the eye.

She gave a tight-lipped smile, the one you make when trying to be polite. He held his breath, feeling a little bummed. She picked up the oxygen tank and helped him strap the buoyancy compensator onto his back, shoulders, and chest. After checking every piece of equipment and the set up twice, she stepped back, her movements and tone impatient.

"All set," she said, putting her hands in the pocket of her jacket.

"Alright," he placed the regulator in his mouth and sat on the side of the boat. Then he fell backward into the sea.

Once he gave her the OK signal, he went down to the bottom of the firth. Isla had been right. The currents were not as strong as the first trip, and the cold layers were more stratified. Once he passed through the thermocline, that was it. There were no other physically-shocking changes in temperature. He was able to focus on investigating the sea floor instead of numb fingers. It was still *very* cold, but he wasn't adjusting his body often to thermal shifts. He just felt the cold the whole time.

Casper was distracted. His eyes were scanning the sand and rocks and sessile critters. His gloved hand dusted off various areas to search for a metallic shine. He only half paid attention to what he was doing and looking at, as his mind partially watched a replay of last night.

Isla had kissed him. It was a drunk kiss, but it happened. It appeared to happen in the mist of an emotional breakdown, so it could be possible that she hadn't meant to press her lips to his and she was reaching out for her own distraction or companionship. She may even regret doing it, and that is partially why she has acted distant the whole morning.

All these possible reasons did not stop the fact that Casper enjoyed the kiss. It wasn't sloppy or wet, though it was a little unsteady as the woman had been inebriated. Still, once she did it, Casper knew he wanted to kiss her back. He wanted to kiss her again, as well as other things. Not only that, he wanted to help her inside, clean her up, and tuck her into her bed. He wanted to care.

He was on a mission, and romance was *not* going to get in his way. Yet, would it be so bad if it did? He found the necklace but what next? Someone may have already dredged up the treasure and never reported it, and Casper was looking for scraps. He had no plan of what to do after this trip as he put his whole faith in Bella's notes. He didn't have the money to do a third trip, and he knew Isla wouldn't be kind enough and take him out for free. He sure as hell didn't want to seduce her for a discount, as tempting as that may be, and possibly easy.

Casper felt guilty for thinking of Isla was "easy," but sometimes she acted desperate. No, that is not the right word. He could sense that she was in a floundering panic in life right now, and she might be easily persuaded to do something that she normally wouldn't agree to, only to take her mind off of her personal troubles and to make her feel good. Who knows, maybe she was already sleeping with other men, or women, and that was her outlet. Maybe she was lying about Bill and actually was in love with him, but was too nervous to go back into a serious relationship.

A tidbit of jealousy puffed through Casper's core, and he bumped into a rock filled with coral. Tiny pieces broke off the rock and floated up and out, away from the solid surface. Casper swam a little faster to get out of the cloud of debris, and he realized he had been swimming in the wrong direction. *Shit.*

Turning left, Casper kept his eye on his compass as he forced himself to watch the ground. He may have missed something and he didn't have time to retrace his steps. All because he thought of the former relationship between Bill and Isla. The way Isla spoke, it sounded as if he was her last relationship. Was he the last person she slept with? Was he good? Maybe that was one of the reasons she broke up with him, because he couldn't satisfy her.

I wonder if I could. Casper thought as he watched the light from his flashlight reveal a small lobster, its claws raised toward the light. As the light passed over more of the floor in front of Casper, he imagined pleasing Isla. His mouth kissing the insides of her thighs, finding his way in between her legs, making her moan.

It was not possible to get hard in a dry suit in forty-degree temperature. Was it?

**

Another soft snore floated through the air of the room, and Casper shut his eyes tight. The same thoughts from before circulated through his mind, and then he started to hear static. White noise. Voices.

Opening his eyes, Casper realized it was the boat's radio. Not the boombox that had broken, but the radio communicating to shore. He sat up and listened, wondering what he should do. Isla was sound asleep, clearly not waking up on her own. He felt bad, but he didn't know how important the message was. If a call came late at night, it probably was serious.

Stepping out of bed, Casper walked on the balls of his foot to Isla's bed. Even though he was about to wake her up, his instinct told him to be quiet.

"Isla?" He whispered, not wanting to jar her awake, "Isla."

The woman's chest rose and fell, still not awake. Casper placed his head on the blanket and shook the bed a little.

"Isla?"

Something slapped against his face, and his cheek began stinging. He stepped back, clutching the area.

"What the *fuck* are *you* doing?" Isla's voice shouted, and he could see the outline of her body sitting up in the bed.

"I was waking you up," he said, his voice raising a little in defense.

"You think you can come onto my boat," the captain was not standing over him, as he had slumped to the floor, and she sounded as if she were ready to hit him again, "And just climb on top of me, you think again! I'm turning this boat to shore and we're going back, and then I'm calling the pol—"

"There was a call on the radio," Casper said, hoping she heard him through her shouting. "I woke you up because it sounded important."

Isla's shadow paused before moving wordlessly to the stairs. The lights came on, and Casper snapped his eyes to see her running up the steps to the main deck. Grabbing his coat, he followed up the stairs and joined her at the sheltered hull.

"This is Isla from the Eimear, over."

"This is Logan," the old man's familiar voice crackled through the radio, "I'm sorry to wake you, but we need you to come back to shore. Someone broke into your house."

"Please repeat," Isla said, though Casper could see from her face that she understood what Logan had said.

"Your father's house has been vandalized," Logan's voice came in more clearly, then became choppy again, "We need you to come back."

Isla paused before responding, "I'm coming home now. Roger."

She turned to Casper, a strange expression on her face. He didn't know what to say, but his first thought was concern for her safety. His second was that his search tomorrow would be delayed.

"I'm so sorry, Casper," Isla said, reaching out and touching his chin so she could see where she had slapped him, "For hitting you, and for cutting the trip short. We have to return early."

"Of course," he said, letting her fingers press against the scruff on his jaw, "You need to deal with this. I can't believe someone would break into your house."

"I agree," she said, turning on all the lights of the boat and bringing the anchor up. "There's nothing of value in the house. Break-ins aren't unheard of, but usually it's kids pulling a prank on a teacher or friend."

With the anchor up, Isla started the boat and turned it west toward the shore. The ocean was dark, with the faintest lights on the horizon from the coastline and other boats. Casper hadn't really observed the sea at night, and staring at it now gave him a mixed feeling. He felt calm and peaceful, but also impending doom. Like something terrible was waiting for him on shore, and he was only safe on the Eimear.

"There's ice packs down below," Isla told him as they stood by the hull, staring out the front window together.

"It doesn't hurt anymore," Casper lied, not wanting her to feel bad about defending herself. He hadn't thought about how scary it must have been to wake up to your large male passenger standing over you at night. "I'm more concerned about tomorrow's trips."

"You can ask Billie to take you out," Isla asked, glancing at him looking forward again, "He does charters, too."

"Yeah, I know," Casper said, *But he requires diving buddies.*

Chapter 30 - Kelsey

The land masses were difficult to see in the fog, so it was not until the morning mist rose up from the sea that the man-o-war was spotted.

"It's British!" shouted Sam, who dangled from one of the mast ropes.

"Not surprised," Mateo said, then peered at Kelsey. "What should we do?"

The captain said nothing for a few moments, squinting out at the monstrously grand ship on the horizon. It was far enough away that it could just be passing through, since they were still in British waters. Man-o-wars were not rare, but still caused the crew to break out in cold sweats and itchy palms. They weren't the most honest merchant sailors, and they did murder and bury the bodies of five British soldiers.

"We keep going south," Kelsey spoke with a calm reassurance, and he noticed Mateo's shoulders relax a little. "As long as the men can keep quiet, we've done nothing wrong."

"What if they search the hull?" Mateo asked, glancing down through the deck's grate. Lines of barrels could barely be seen in the dull sun.

"We'll deal with what we're given," Kelsey scanned the deck, gauging the attitude of the crew. "Tell the men not to accelerate, nor veer course. Let me know if the British approach."

Nodding, Mateo started shouting orders. Kelsey found his son helping pull a piece of canvas to repair a sail.

"David," Kelsey said, giving the other men a tight grin. "Come to the cabin when you've finished."

Kelsey's boots clicked sharply toward his quarters, and when he entered the office, he shut the door and let out a slow breath. There was a thick rot in the pit of his stomach, the same sensation he felt before he left the port.

Just as the silence was turning stale, Kelsey heard the doorknob turn. David entered the room with a curious grin. His shirt stuck to his skin with sweat, and his face was red.

"Come," Kelsey stepped over to his desk and unlocked one of the drawers. "Over here."

The boy met his father on the other side of the desk. In Kelsey's hand was a silver locket, with intricate metalwork on the outer clasps. A long thin chain looped through the clasp hoop, awaiting to be equipped.

"This was your mother's," Kelsey opened the locket and showed a tiny enamel painting of a woman with long black curls and fair skin. "Well, it's mine, given to me by your mother."

"Who is that?" David asked, pointing at the painting.

"Who do you think it is?"

"My mother."

Kelsey nodded and placed the open locket into David's hands. "I want you to have it."

"Why?" The boy blurted, but then blushed. "Thank you kindly, father, but why?"

"I've stared at it for so long," Kelsey shrugged, closing and locking the drawer, "I don't need it anymore. Not that I needed it in the first place to remember what she looked like."

David waved his thumb through the air, as if he wanted to brush the picture but didn't want to ruin it. "Is it because of the British ship?"

Damn, this boy. "No. This is something I should've done a year or two ago. Here's the thing, David; we never know what will happen in a day, or a year. We should be prepared for what God brings us, and you need to be ready. I need to prepare you for when I'm not here, as well as give you what is rightfully yours."

Kelsey wrapped his hands around David's, helping close the clasp. The boy's fingers were cold to the touch.

"Don't wear this around your neck," Kelsey continued, "Don't let anyone else know you have this, even Mateo."

"Why?" David asked, his eyebrows furrowing.

"You can't trust a sailor," Kelsey grinned, laughing at his own irony. "Especially when he's your dearest partner. Keep it hidden with your belongings. Don't ever take it out in public."

"Because it's valuable?"

"Yes," Kelsey nodded, then tilted his head to the side. "And the design is Spanish, and of an era and style that the British may look down upon. If they catch you with this, they may question you."

"What should I say?" David asked. "If they catch me?"

"That you found it," Kelsey cleared his throat, "And that you are British. You have a good accent, right?"

"Yes, sir," David pulled out his best street urchin phrase he learned while spending time at the English ports. "My name is David Smith, and I'm from Birmingham."

Kelsey couldn't help from laughing at the spot on but awful accent, but then he heard footsteps clatter toward the door and a heavy knocking. David rushed to his bed and shoved the locket into the grimest bag he had.

"Come in," Kelsey stood up and made himself look as if he was tidying the books on his desk.

Sam opened the door wide, concern lining his forehead. "The British ship is catching up."

Chapter 31 - Isla

Isla could barely think about the waves crashing into the bow of the Eimear as she sped across the sea toward land. She needed to get to her father's house and figure out what was taken. It was a long drive back to shore and she knew she probably should have waited until sunrise to launch full-speed in the pitch dark of the Firth, especially with a customer on board, but all she could feel was her heart in her throat. Instead of the distance spinning warning of the lighthouse's beam, she saw some unknown figure in a black mask stealing through her home.

It wasn't until a warm blanket fell over her shoulders that Isla realized she was shivering. Glancing behind her, she saw Casper standing there, his hands falling to his sides.

"Thank you," she said, using one hand to pull the edges of the blanket tight against her chest, blocking the heat inside.

"Is there anything else you need?" he asked, his voice comforting.

"No," she didn't even shake her head in response as she kept her stare forward, "I'm all set, Casper."

She heard his footsteps as he went downstairs, and she let out a heavy sigh. There were so many emotions stirring up adrenaline in her blood, she didn't even know what to mentally sort through first. All of yesterday had been awkward between Casper and her. While he acted nonchalant and confident, she was blundering and spiteful. She hadn't been able to look him in the eye, and during the quiet moments during lunch and dinner, all she could feel was the heat in her cheeks and Casper's eyes on her neck.

She was able to forget about it when she went to sleep. Then, she woke up to the large American hovering over her. At first she had thought it was the mysterious entity that her father warned her about in his note. Before then, the idea of some danger lurking in her father's past had slept in the back of Isla's head. When she saw Casper's dark form, she immediately thought it was the very thing that had killed her father. Whatever it was, spirit or human.

After defending herself from Casper's advances, then learning he had only been waking her up because of an emergency call from Logan, Isla felt herself fall further into the pit of awkward despair. These feelings coincided with the anxiety, anger, and fear of learning about someone breaking into her house. Therefore, her skin felt as if a group of bees were trapped under her skin and beating their wings, trying to get out. Her chest was tight and, even though she could breath, needed to remind herself to not make shallow inhalations. *Don't hold your breath.*

When the Eimear reached the dock, Isla could see Logan standing outside the boathouse, waiting for her. As she silded the bat along the dock and tied it up, Logan came down the aisle with the cart.

"I can help your diver unpack," he told Isla, climbing over the side and onto the deck. "And cooling down the lass."

His calloused, veiny hand patted the wall surrounding the helm.

"I can do it." Even though she trusted the old man to do it, Isla had always done the post-trip chores by herself. "Thank you for bringing the cart."

"There's a cruiser in the lot," Logan said, unstrapping the diving equipment and beginning to carry items to the cart. "To escort you back to your place."

"Escort me?" Isla asked just as Casper ascended the stairs with his belongings. "Why?"

"Hi there," Logan nodded to Casper before looking back at the woman, "They don't know who broke into your place or why. They need you to check to see if anything is missing. They also don't want the person to come back."

"Why would they come back?" Isla asked, though she felt as if she already knew.

Logan gave her a knowing look, as if he didn't want to say the answer out loud, either. Casper, who had finished loading the cart with equipment, stood on the wooden dock, staring at the two Scots.

"I've got all the stuff," Casper gestured to the cart, "But is there any way I can help, Isla?"

Blushing, Isla looked away from Logan's eyes and at Casper. "If you can come swing by my place later today for the refund, I'll have it ready most likely in the afternoon."

"Refund?" Casper asked, sounding confused.

As Logan busied himself with cleaning up the boat, Isla stepped onto the dock and looked up at Casper's eyes.

"Delaying your trip is not your fault," Isla explained, attempting to sound business-like and not as if she had drunk-kissed him less than forty-eight hours before. "You gave me a deposit and the full fee, and you dived the first day. You still had two more days to dive, so I will return the money for those two days."

"Isla," Casper's eyebrows furrowed, looking surprised as well as if he was about to laugh, "You're dealing with an emergency. Don't worry about me right now, or about paying me back. We can speak about this in a few days when you've sorted things out."

"I don't think I'll have this sorted out in a few days," Isla grinned but felt sour inside. "And I have a feeling you aren't talking about the money... we really should keep this professional."

"I'm speaking to you as a friend," Casper said, stepping back. He paused before chuckling. "You know, screw it. I like you, Isla, and I would like to see you again. I don't care about our *professional* relationship, and I would like to take you out again."

Blood turning cold, Isla stared at the blonde man. Her words were stuck in her throat, and she watched as he stepped closer to her, his hand reaching for her arm.

"Next time," Casper lowered his voice, his finger gentle and warm on her warm, "I hope I have the guts to get drunk and spill my heart out to you. Then we'll be even."

Letting go of her arm, Casper stepped behind the cart and pushed it up the dock. Isla turned toward the Eimear and saw Logan walking up the stairs. She stepped onto the main deck and could see the tight grin on his lips.

"Don't say anything," she growled, grabbing her bags from his grip.

"Mhmm," he put his hands in his pocket and grunted. "Even if you do go out with him, I'd still give him his money back. You don't want to owe anyone anything."

"Except you," Isla grinned, "I'll always be in debt with you, Logan. Sure you can take care of the rest?"

"Been sure for fifty years."

"Alright," Isla ran a hand through her messy hair, "I'll call you later with details. Good night."

"Good *morning*, actually," Logan nodded at the thin line of yellow on the horizon above the hills.

Rolling her eyes, Isla made her way to her truck and let the police officer follow her home.

Chapter 32 - Casper

The very same day that he reached land, Casper asked Bill about his charter service. He had to do something, be active, instead of thinking about what he had said to Isla. What he had confessed.

That morning, when Isla rushed the Eimear eastward to the docks, Casper had felt an overwhelming sense of concern and protection. Someone tried to harm her, or at least upset her. Even though he wasn't local, Casper knew break-ins didn't happen here. A small part of him wondered if it was Bill, another reason why Casper wanted to work with the dive shop owner.

"Is she alright?" Bill asked on the phone, borrowed from Marie at the bed and breakfast. Casper had left all the equipment at Logan's boathouse and went to his rental. When Billy Bob's opened, he called to schedule a trip. All Bill could talk about though was Isla.

"She is safe," Casper said, not really knowing if his words were true. "There were cops with her, and she's a tough girl."

There was a pause on the line and Casper thought he may have sounded more connected to the woman. Even though he had expressed his feelings to Isla, he didn't want the whole town to know. He doubted Isla wanted that, too, no matter what her decision would be. If her feelings were reciprocated, she would want a quiet romance. If she didn't feel the same way, she would want the situation to die out, unnoticed.

"Back to the point," Casper said, breaking the silence through the phone, "There are specific locations I need to go to, as I am conducting scientific field work."

"That's all good but you need a buddy," Bill responded, his tone serious but still friendly. "I'm not sure if we can find someone so soon who would want to pair up."

"Why don't you dive with me?" Casper asked, glancing up from the front desk as Marie walked in with a warm smile.

"I have to watch the boat," Bill said, matter-of-fact. "I'll ask around and see if anyone wants to join."

"No, no," Casper spoke quickly then took a short breath. "It's okay. I will think of something. Give me today to plan some things and I'll call you back."

"Let me know what you need," Bill said, sounding tired. "Though you need a partner."

After saying good-bye, Casper hung the phone up and gripped the desk.

"Everything okay, dear?" Marie asked, her warm eyes gazing up at him.

"Yes," he nodded, smiling at her and standing up straight. "My trip has been delayed. I need someone to join me while I scuba dive."

"Och," Marie made a sharp, guttural Scottish grunt, laughing a little. "There's a couple in room two who were debating on diving. Shall I ask them?"

"Sure," Casper nodded, not really aware of any other options he had. He had to find the treasure, but he couldn't find it with strangers. As Marie left the room and creaked down the hallway, Casper went through all the possible solutions to this insane plan.

A group of footsteps came down the hallway, and Marie entered. Behind her were two short dark-haired people, a man and a woman. They both appeared to be in their mid-twenties, wearing fashionably comfortable clothes. Their smiles stretched wide, and their eyes grew big when they saw Casper.

"This is the scientist I told you about," Marie told them, gesturing to Casper. "He is in need of friends for his dive."

"We would love to join you," the man said, his English thick with a Greek accent. "If that is possible."

"We only dived in Crete and Morocco," the woman said, her accent equally accented, as she clutched the man's arm. "But we want to try the colder waters."

"This is great news," Casper faked excitement, holding his hand out to shake each of theirs. "Let me call the dive shop and let him know. We should go there to pick out equipment, dry suits and such."

As Casper picked up the telephone receiver, the couple ran back to their rooms.

"Hi, Bill?" Casper said into the phone. "It's Casper. I found not one, but *two* dive buddies."

**

The Greek couple, whose names were Adar and Cyrus, had rented a car, so drove Casper to the dive shop. They parked by the curb outside of the shop and walked in, and the couple stared in amazement at the collection of items. Sorting through a rack of snorkels, Bill poked his head up and grinned.

"Your luck is pretty high, my friend," Bill told Casper as he walked around the rack and approached the group. He held his hand out to the couple. "My name's Bill, and I'll be assisting you."

After the greetings and pleasantries, Bill provided paperwork for Adara and Cyrus for the trip, and then helped them try on dry suits. Casper knew the preparations would take a while, so he stepped out to the street and headed to the coffee shop.

Each morning at the bed and breakfast, Marie provided basic black coffee. Not bad but not great. Casper didn't want to constantly buy a five dollar latte, but his brain needed a boost. He hadn't slept well last night due to the various ongoings with Isla, and he had been running around all morning planning the back-up trip. Not to mention the stress from worrying about finding the damn treasure.

There were two people in line when Casper opened the door. There were a few older women sitting at a middle table, sipping their drinks and talking about an upcoming local celebration. When Casper came into their view, the women hushed for a minute as they looked at him head to toe. Then they began giggling, returning to their conversation. Casper didn't pay attention but could still feel their gaze every so often.

"Hi," Casper smiled at the young man at the register, "I'll have one medium latte, skim milk, with some room at the top."

He used his credit card to purchase the drink, and walked to the open area on the other side of the counter to wait for the drink. Over the women's gossiping and the steaming of milk foam, he could hear light folk music playing on the speakers. There were fiddles, a banjo, and another instrument he couldn't pick out. There was also a subtle Gaelic voice mixing with the instruments.

The barista placed his drink on the counter and Casper gladly accepted it. He brought it to the other little counter that held all the straws, sugars, and creamers. Picking up two pink non-sweetener packets, he tore the side of each with one rip, and poured the white fake sugar into his drink. Looking out at the window behind the counter, Casper's eyes scanned the street. It was a normal day in town, with children getting out of school and adults taking their afternoon breaks.

There was a person walking on the sidewalk on the opposite side of the coffee, heading southward. Casper's eyes grew wide and almost tipped his coffee over as he recognized the neatly-trimmed brown beard, the short brown hair that began to curl at the tips, the long confident stride of the man. It was him. It had to be Liam.

A grocery truck drove in front of Casper's line of sight, and when the truck passed, the man had disappeared. Shaking his head, Casper stirred his coffee and walked toward the door. Before he left the coffee shop, he checked the street once more for the man. Even though he kept telling himself it was his imagination, he couldn't ignore the chill grazing down his spine.

Chapter 33 - Kelsey

In a few short hours, the British warship had used the full power of its sharp white sails to catch up to the Crooked Stock. It was unnerving watching the brown spec of dirt become a towering beast, fully knowing what was to come. Kelsey knew what would happen. He also knew he needed a plan, and for the first time in all his years of being a captain, he didn't have one.

"Mateo," Kelsey pulled the younger sailor away from the crowded first deck, where the crew were running around, preparing for a battle.

"I know that face," Mateo's eyes were wide with apprehension. "What are our chances?"

Looking around, Kelsey checked for anyone listening in. "Low. At best, I'll be charged for piracy."

"That's the best?" Mateo let out a humorless laugh. "What's the worst?"

"Treason," Kelsey spoke with a grim face.

Mateo's smirk faded. "What did you do?"

Shaking his head, Kelsey ignored the question. "I need you to take David and a few supplies to shore. Remember that small inlet we camped on, when we were traveling north? It's coming up soon."

"I won't be able to get back to you," Mateo said, confused by the orders. "The Crooked Stock will have sailed past by then."

"That's why we're lowering the anchor," Kelsey explained as if he had told Mateo this insane plan before, "We'll never outrun the man o'war, so we have to face it. We can reason with them."

"Why take David to shore, then?" Mateo asked.

"You're also taking the chest," Kesey whispered, "From Laird Thomas."

The first mate was silent again.

"Can you do that?" Kelsey raised an eyebrow, feeling a little lightheaded from the heat of the situation.

"Yes, sir," Mateo gave a nod. "What about the men?"

"I'll tell them that we're allowing the British to search the ship," Kelsey explained, "We have nothing to hide."

"Well…" Mateo gave a sideways glance toward the floorboards.

"Like I said before," Kelsey stepped closer, "As long as the men can keep their mouths shut, we'll be safe. Start preparations with David."

Two men carried the chest out to one of the rowboats. David and Mateo carried a few bags of food and other supplies, and stowed them in the back of the tiny vessel. A small crowd had formed around it as Mateo settled in the middle seat. Hesitant to leave, David stood at the port side, staring up at his father.

"We'll have a discussion with the soldiers," Kelsey said, smiling, "Then you'll come back to join us."

"What happens if they search for us on shore?" David asked, looking at the ship that was still too far to see any indication of purpose.

"They won't see you heading there if you leave now," Kelsey waved his son toward the boat, and David stepped over the side. "Listen to Mateo, you hear?"

With a serious, childlike expression, David nodded and gripped the wooden seat underneath him. Jonesy and Ruben lowered the rowboat down, and soon Kelsey couldn't see his son's face over the side of the ship. He didn't bend over the railing to see David, but instead turned and faced the men of his crew.

"I understand your concerns," Kelsey projected his voice, no longer feeling the waver in his voice. "We all have a past of the British. Being here, in the waters of Scotland, was a risk we all partook when you joined this crew. Still, we have a chance to leave with our lives, if not our goods. Speak little, act little, when those redcoats step foot on our planks."

There was a small murmur in the crowd, but no one appeared defiant. No one was happy, but they were eager to listen to the captain, trusting he knew best with how to stay alive. The men returned to their useless preparations and prayers. As the warship came into range to see the bright red, white, and blue colors, Kelsey allowed himself one glance to shore.

Mateo was pulling the row boat behind a large boulder. David was already out of sight from the sea. They both would be safe and hidden, as well as the chest.

The weight of a stone lifted from Kelsey's shoulders. They would survive this. They would move on. The crew would be fine. He would bring David back to—

A loud ear-cracking boom rocked the Crooked Stock, and Kelsey gripped the railing on the portside to see smoke escape one of the portholes of one of the cannons. The steaming ball landed a few meters away from the warship. That's when the British decided to turn sideways.

"They're coming for us!" Mariano shouted, and Kelsey's blood ran cold.

Chapter 34 - Isla

Isla's father's house had been intimidating when arriving three months ago. Walking in after a burglary made the interior frightening to observe. The lock to the front door was busted. The three police officers on the scene reported that the door was left open wide. They said that while the house was a mess, nothing valuable appeared to be missing. When arriving early that morning, Isla checked the jewellery in her mother's forgotten box, up in her father's old bedroom. The small television in the living room still sat on a table by the back wall. In the living room, kitchen, upstairs hallway, and closet, the documents and books that had been once stacked knee-high were spilled across the hardwood floor and rugs. This was bad enough, but when Isla saw the work she had done in the study was destroyed, she felt light headed.

"Is there anything missing?" One of the officers asked, holding a small notepad and a pen.

"It doesn't appear so," Isla ran her hand through her hair, glaring at the mounds of parchment in front of her feet. "I mean, what were they looking for?"

"Do you have any enemies?" The officer asked, her words cautious. "Someone who might want to hurt you."

"No," Isla shook her head, "This is my father's house, anyways. I've just been organizing it after his death."

Nodding, the officer glanced around the room. She must have been the first person in town to see what the inside looked like, and undoubtedly would report her observations to other townsfolk.

"What about your father?"

"Everyone loved Fredrick Muir," Isla couldn't help but grin, and noticed the officer doing the same. "No one would harm him."

The officer took a deep breath, as if she wanted to speak freely. "Do you have some friends you can stay with?"

"Why?" Isla asked, putting her hands on her hips, still staring at the mess.

"The person who did this might come back," the officer said, putting her notepad away in her coat pocket. "There weren't any other break-ins on this street. They were looking for something, and may return to find it."

Like me? Were they looking for me? Isla swallowed the lump in her throat and poured herself a small glass of whiskey.

"Want some?" Isla asked out of habit, not wanting to be rude.

"Can't on the job," the officer held a hand up in refusal, "But thanks."

"Right, sorry," Isla sipped the liquid before returning to the conversation. "I'll stay here. Need to clean everything, anyways."

"We'll post an officer out on the street," the officer stepped out of the study and Isla followed. "Call us if anything strange happens. I'd get that lock fixed today, if you can."

"Will do," Isla had been ready to open the front door, but there was no need as it was still left ajar. "Thank you for your help."

The officer exited through the front door and joined the other officers on the sidewalk. They glanced back at Isla, who didn't look away from the trio while downing the rest of her whiskey. It was only nine thirty in the morning, and she needed a second drink.

Closing the front door, Isla placed a heavy book up against the wooden slab so it would stay shut. The house was cold from being open all morning, and the alcohol wasn't warming Isla up fast enough. She turned the heat on and pulled on another sweater, then called the locksmith. Frank, one of two locksmiths in town, would swing by on his way home and fix the front door. At least Isla could sleep a little better tonight, with a new lock and a cop car outside.

Then she went to the study and sorted through the mixed up papers. She stacked them into the two piles, useful and unuseful, but the piles were less straight and organized than when she previously had done. Once she could see the floor, she went to the living room and did the same. This process was longer as she hadn't touched this room at all before the break-in, so there were stacks of novels for entertainment, as well as year-old bills and magazines. She dumped all the magazines and bills into a balck trash bag and put all the novels against the wall by the doorframe. This took most of the day.

Isla finished the living room just as a knock sounded on the front door. *Franks here early.* Toeing the book out of the way, she opened the door.

"Hi!" Chlose stood head to toe in a white skirt suit, three-inch heels, and hair pulled perfectly into a bun. Manicured hands clutched a brown paper bag, though Isla couldn't see inside.

"Hey?" Isla wasn't intoxicated but had been slowly emptying the bottle of whiskey in her father's study all day, and she knew she wouldn't be able to fake a smile.

"How are you?" Chloe asked, peaking in around the half-open door. "I heard about what happened."

"How would you expect me to be, Chloe?" Isla said simply, her tone not harsh but definitely not friendly. "I can't even close my door all the way."

The poised woman said nothing for a moment. "I actually came here to see if you need help. To alleviate any stress."

Thinking back to her teenage years, Isla remembered her and Chloe hanging out every lunch period, every day after school, running around town and the shops, driving out to the fields and cliffs. They had been best friends for most of Isla's youth, but now they felt like strangers.

"You can come in," Isla opened the door all the way, letting Chloe enter before closing it and returning the book to its spot. "I just finished the two front rooms."

"What do you dread the most?" Chloe asked, hanging her purse on the hook in the hallway.

"What?" Isla asked, thinking how bold and thought-provoking the question was, and wondering how to answer it.

"What room is the worst?" Chloe asked, pointing down the hallway. "I can start on whatever you don't want to."

"Oh," Isla stepped toward the kitchen and nodded toward the door frame. "This is pretty bad, but so is upstairs."

There were still dirty dishes in the sink from days ago, maybe weeks. Isla hadn't even cleaned out the pantry from when her father still lived here. It was disgusting, she knew. But she wasn't going to say it outloud.

"I'll start here," Chloe said, taking her coat off and draping it over the back of a chair. "I'll make dinner, too."

"No need for a casserole," Isla gave a grim laugh, thinking of the pile of casserole dishes right after her father's funeral.

Chloe set the brown paper bag on the counter. "How about cheeseburgers and chips?"

Those beautiful French manicured fingers pulled two take-out boxes from the bag, and placed them on a cleared spot on the table. The greasy smell of food wrapped around Isla, and she grinned.

"Won't you stain your costume?" Isla cleared more space on the table and opened one of the boxes.

"I have others," Chloe sat down in one of the empty chairs and began picking at her own pile of potato fries.

"How'd you know I needed this?" Isla asked, biting into the juicy cheeseburger.

"This is what we always got after exams," Chloe said with a mouth full of fries. "The best food for stress. Am I wrong?"

Shaking her head, Isla felt the buttered carbs melt on her tongue and fill her empty stomach. She hadn't eaten since dinner the previous night, and whiskey could only keep her going for a few hours. The house felt warmer, and she felt less worried as the night went on.

Chapter 35 - Casper

Lying to the Greek couple was not difficult for Casper, and continuing his search for the treasure was also not difficult. He helped Adara and Cyrus gear up, and vice versa, and then he fell back into the ocean first. Once all three scuba divers gave Bill the "OK" hand signal, they deflated their buoyancy compensator little by little. The weight of their gear, bodies, and belts pulled them through the saltwater slowly, following the anchor attached to the Makenna Wild. When Caser felt his knees brush against the rocky benthics, he took a deep breath.

The nice thing about being underwater is not having to speak. The less he had to tell the couple, the better. They balanced awkwardly a few inches above the bottom, their hands clutching their regulator, computer, flashlight. They had the beginner diving jitters, and the bubbles that escaped their regulator were more frequent than Casper's exhales.

They both stared at Casper with waiting, needy eyes. Casper made a gesture to them, reminding them to calm their bodies and slow their breathing. While they both nodded and gave the "OK" signal, the speed and number of bubbles did not change.

Taking up his compass, Casper changed his direction so he was facing west. Bill had anchored the boat directly over the coordinates Casper had provided, but the area was still large and Casper needed to start somewhere. He would do a sweep on this part of the ship, panning back after doing a little arc north. Tomorrow, he would search the other side of the boat, head east, and do a little arc south before returning. After speaking with Adara and Cyrus, he didn't worry about them noticing his activity. Both had large waterproof cameras, and as Casper led them west along the seafloor, their eyes rarely turned away from the critters and colorful substrates.

After twenty minutes of diving, the three divers began to enter an area with high vegetation. Seaweeds and kelps spiraled up from their base in the rocky sand. It reminded Casper of the dive he went on and bumped into the seal. Hopefully nothing would jump out of the green-tinted shadows as the less experienced divers would most likely did something stupid.

There were a few times where Casper looked back and didn't see the couple. Then he would spot their flashlights coming around a trunk of algae, and he would exhale deeply. Paying attention to other divers while keeping an eye out for treasure was annoying and frustrating, but Casper didn't have a choice. Part of his mind was focused on any shiny objects or odd, man-made shapes jutting through the sand or overgrown corals and algae. Then he would remember that he wasn't alone, and divert his eyes to his companions. Another reason he didn't want to dive with a buddy.

As Casper and the couple began swimming north in a curving direction, a large boulder came into view. There was an excess of small animals compared to the rest of the sea floor, which meant there may be a higher mineral content. Adara pointed at her camera and then at the rock, and Casper nodded. As the couple began photographing tiny creatures in the crevices, edging around the hard surface, Casper started swimming around the opposite side. He would meet them in a few minutes and they would continue their path back to the boat.

Alone, Casper scanned the holes and seemingly-unnatural shapes of the structure. His flashlight would light up the tiny bright eyes of crustaceans, and the wiry legs would scitter the tiny shrimp-like bodies back into their homes. Fish came up to Casper's drysuit and would try nibbling on the fabric, curious to see if he was edible.

Something dark caught Casper's attention. It was at the base of the rock, poking out from under a pile of coarse sand. Deflating his buoyancy compensator, Casper reached his gloved hand out to the pile. Dusting some sand away, he began to see a point right-corner, appearing to be made of a wooden material. The corner reached out into x-, y-, and z-axis directions. The corner of a box.

Holding your breath underwater is not recommended, but Casper hadn't moved from his position as his eyes were glued to what he found. Sucking a huge gulp of air through his regulator, he looked around his surroundings for the other divers. Still alone. He took a picture of the corner, which would record the exact GPS coordinates of where to return later. This was it! This was really it!

It took Casper a minute to control his breathing. He met Adara and Cyrus at the other side of the rock and pointed at his oxygen level and watch, which suggested he was running low. They seemed pretty reluctant to leave, too, but they followed Casper east. The whole twenty minutes back to the boat, Casper's thought ran wild.

I found it. Bella was right. I actually found the treasure! How will I dig it out? It looks pretty big and stuck in the sand, and some of that sand looks solidified. I'll have to return with Isla, but then I'll have to tell her. I don't know if I can trust her. Not yet. I definitely can't trust bIll or these two.

The iron loops of the anchor appeared in front of Casper, and he waved for the other two divers to surface first. They all took decompression stops at specific points on the anchor, holding onto the metal rope so the current wouldn't sweep them away. Finally, they were all on board, eager to equip their soaked heavy attire.

"I'll change last," Casper told the couple, helping Bill strapp the used oxygen tanks into a cabinet.

"Thank you!" Cyrus said, still breathing heavily from fatigue. "For showing us the beauty of the sea. You should start a touring business."

"Oh, thanks," Casper nodded, sounding half-interested in the conversation. He felt fuzzy, as if his body wasn't even fully present on the Makenna Wild with wind biting as his damp hair and skin.

"You really could make some money here," Bill said after the couple went below deck. "I don't come out here as often as I'd like, but we could team up. I drive the boat, you give dive tours."

"I'm not certified for that," Casper said, hanging up his drysuit on a rack. "And I don't plan on staying in Scotland for long."

"Really?" There was an odd tone in Bill's voice, like a combination of relief but loneliness. "That's a shame."

"Also, if possible," Casper said, "Can we go to a different location than what I gave you before? I think they're better coordinates."

"Sure thing," Bill smiled, bringing the anchor up. "Just let me know and I'll start the engine."

The coordinates were actually closer to land, about eight miles off shore. They were also completely unnecessary as Casper really wanted to end the dive sooner. He didn't need to search any other location, so if they could just return to shore after the last dive tomorrow, that would suit Casper's plans very well. He needed to figure out how he was going to return. Alone.

After giving Bill the coordinates, Casper went down to the cabinet and changed into warm, dry clothes. The couple were playing a card game at the table, and a pot of water was boiling on the stove.

"We're making pasta," Cyrus said, not looking away from his hand of cards, "Do you want some, Mr. Shaw?"

"No, I'm going to do some reading, maybe go to sleep early," Casper ran a hand through his hair, already drying. "And call me Casper, please."

"Good night, Casper," Adarasaid, her white teeth glistening from the dim light of the table's lamp.

Unlike Isla's sleeping quarters, Bill had rooms. The boat was a little bigger, so there were four rooms below deck. The first room was where the divers could lounge, play games, and watch television on the small box set. The kitchenette was also set on the side of the first room. The second room was the small bathroom, which still did not have a shower but had a bit more room to move around in. Then there were the two sleeping rooms. The couple took one, and Bill and Casper took the other. Since Bill was steering the boat, Casper had privacy once he closed the thin door to the bedroom.

The first thing Casper did was examine the photo he took with his camera. The quality wasn't great with the low light under the water, but he could make out the details of the wooden corner. In the bottom right corner were the GPS coordinates, and Casper recorded the numbers in his notebook. Bella's notebook.

He didn't need her notes anymore, but still reviewed them once more before going to sleep. He felt as if finding the box was a trick, and the memory or the opportunity would slip away. He still was unsure of his next steps, though when he really thought about it, he didn't have a plan from after he discovered the treasure. He just wanted to find it, and now he thinks he has.

Casper fell asleep to the rumbling of the boat, gliding through choppy waves. He didn't wake up when the Greek couple stumbled to their room. He didn't wake up when the boat slowed to a stop, nor when the anchor landed into the water and made a chink noise when it snagged a rock on the sea floor. He didn't wake up when Bill went to sleep.

The thing that woke Casper up was the smell of smoke.

Chapter 36 - Kelsey

Hearing the first cannon go off underneath Kelsey's feet was surprising, but when the thick trunks of the railing a few feet away exploded, he found himself descending into a state of shock. Splinters burst out from the impact, which also caused the Crooked Stock to shift backwards from the push of the cannonball.

"Shall we continue the attack?" Mateo asked the captain.

"Continue?" Kelsey asked, looking from the British war ship to his smaller merchant vessel. "We weren't supposed to attack."

"What're we to do?" Mariano asked, panic in his tone.

Looking around at the crewmembers, he saw the fear in their face. Despite their hard pasts, they never have had to deal with an event such as this. This was the British, coming at them hard and direct.

"We fight," Kelsey ordered, standing up a little straighter. "This is our ship, and we will not run from our troubles, will we?"

"No!" Shouted the men.

"We take care of our woman!" Kelsey patted one of the masts of the ship, feeling the solid material under his fingers. "Since she has taken care of us! We go down with her, or so call us cowards. Load the cannons! Arm yourselves and prepare for death, for we'll be greeted with warm arms."

This was the type of speech a leader made when he had barely heard many influential speeches in his life and didn't know what else to say. All he understood was he needed to keep the men's morale up, as well as his own. No right captain could jump over the side and swim to shore, not until the Crooked Stock was gone, at least.

All the crew went down below to grab swords and pistols, but only half returned to the main deck. The other half readied the cannons, and when three more cannonballs slammed into the side of the mechant vessel, four balls from below spit out toward the British. Kelsey heard the balls make contact, the crack of wood echoing across the surface of the water.

The merchant vessel called the Crooked Stock would never have lasted, no matter who was captain, who was sailor, or who was God. Kelsey knew the ship would not survive the full brunt of the British man-o'war, though survival did not matter. Fighting back mattered.

In a few short minutes, hard floorboards no longer held Kelsey's body above the water. The cold sting of Scottish waters rose up to his chest, and he kept his arms stretched out on either side of his torso. He kicked his leather boots off to decrease the drag, and this allowed him to keep his chin above the waves. Pieces of broken ship floated around him, as well as fellow crewmates.

"Capt'n!" Jonesy called, gurgling saltwater. "Help!"

The younger man was thrashing on the surface, unable to keep himself above the waves in a calm tread. Kelsey kicked over to the man, bringing along a piece of driftwood.

"Grab on!" Kelsey shouted, aggressively grabbing Jonesy's arm and draping it over the driftwood. "Don't let go of this and kick toward that inlet over there!"

"I can't swim!" Jonesy cried, his eyes wide and red.

"Listen to me, man!" Kelsey shouted, grabbing the man's shoulder roughly. "All you do is kick, or you will die."

Jonesy met Kelsey's eye, paused, and nodded. As he kicked in the direction toward the shore, Kelsey scanned the waters. Everyone else was dead, either from cannon ball, fire, or drowning. One surprising fact that always confused Kelsey was the number of sailors who didn't know how to swim. One would think having the ability to swim would come in handy one day, such as in situations like this. It didn't matter, now, though, as the British warship slowly approached the burning waterlogged debris.

Turning toward the coastline, Kelsey began swimming. He cupped his hands and pulled the water out from in front of him, paddle by paddle, edging closer to the hidden inlet that protected his son.

It took some time to reach the shore. Kelsey's body hurt from the attack, bruises beginning to spread under his skin. His lips were chattering from the chilly sea. He reached a spot where the color of the water changed, shifting to a lighter blue, indicating the increasing shallow bottom. To the right and left of the sandy inlet were sharp rocks. Above them were the classic Scottish cliffs, rising twenty or more feet above the waves.

The tip of Kelsey's toes brushed against the grainy seafloor, but he still had to tread as the waves pushed and pulled at his body. A white object caught his eyesight, and he looked to the left and saw Jonesy's blouse. The man had indeed been able to reach shallow waters, but the sea brought him to the deadly jagged boulders below the cliffs.

Kelsey swam a little bit faster as he expected sharks had detected the blood in the water.

Chapter 37 - Isla

The house was completely clean once Chloe arrived. It took two days, one bottle of whiskey, and about ten black trash bags, as well as two trips to the library donation bin with Isla's pickup truck. After all the work and help, the weight was gone from Isla's chest. The floor could be seen in every room, and the only books that remained were on the bookshelves in the living room and on her father's desk. Isla still wanted to figure out what he was researching, so she kept the materials that she deemed important.

"This really is a beautiful house," Chloe said, sliding her coat on. When she had returned the second day, she arrived wearing a designer tracksuit. Something to be comfortable in, but still make a statement. "Do you have a lawnmower?"

"I think it's broken," Isla said, following CHloe to the front door. "It's in the shed out back; the next thing I need to clean out."

"Little by little, this place will start to look like it used to," Chloe smiled and placed her hand on Isla's arm. "Let me know if you need any help."

"Chloe?" Isla asked, then paused.

"Yes?" Chloe stepped onto the front stairs but kept her eyes on Isla.

"Selling this house..." Isla said, "Will it be hard?"

Her friend's eyes grew big before a large smile spread on her lips. "Want me to talk to Alex about it?"

"Sure," Isla nodded and placed both her hands on her door.

"Bye, now," Chloe descended the stairs, waving.

"Bye, Chloe," Isla said, "Thank you, again."

Closing the door, Isla locked it with the new doorknob. She also turned the deadbolt that she had Frank install. It made her feel safer, especially now that the house felt empty and big without all the clutter. Turning to the living room, she looked at the vacuumed carpet. It had been orange the whole time and completely forgot until the books and papers were removed. As she stared at it now, she realized how ugly the orange was.

The drying washing beeped in the back room, so Isla went and pulled the fresh load out. Many of her mother's old flannels were found in the upstairs closet, so Isla wanted to wash them before giving them away. Though as she folded them, stackin them neatly on top of the dryer, she couldn't resist bringing each one to her chest and smelling the fabric. It no longer smelled like her mother, nor her father, but she imagined her mother wearing these while gardening and going about the town. There was one button-down in particular that Isla remembered her mother wearing. It was a dark green checkered with a lighter forest green, with blocks of royal blue. Maroon bits lined each checker piece. The colors of her clan. While Isla and her father didn't pay much attention to Scottish culture and heritage and clans, Islas mother had taken pride in her ancestors. She even kept her maiden name to preserve her clan: Ruthven. While most people found this stupid and untraditional, Isla's father said he loved her mother even more because of this. A woman who wasn't going to let anyone, especially a man, take away who she was, even in marriage.

That's who Isla wanted to be, though she suspected she would be alone forever.

Pulling the flannel on over her t-shirt, Isla smiled as the warmth spread along her arms and back. As she finished folding the rest of the flannels, there was a knock on the door.

The *back* door.

Body frozen, Isla felt the air in her lungs turn to ice. The lights were on in all the downstairs rooms, except her father's study. The sun had set less than an hour ago, but there were no lights in her backyard. The yard was fenced off, the only gate locked.

Grabbing the sharpest knife from the kitchen, Isla stepped toward the back door. She wished she had asked Frank to install a deadbolt for this door, too. She wished she didn't live alone. She wished she wasn't so *afraid*.

There was another knock, brisk and loud. Isla hid the knife behind her back and used one finger to pull the white curtain away from the small window in the door. A tall masculine figure stood outside, slouched over. It was unknown if this person was armed, or who he was.

"Isla, it's me!" Casper's voice came through the door. "It's Casper Shaw!"

Closing the curtain, Isla took a step back. *What the fuck?*

"What do you want?" Isla shouted through the door, looking for her cellphone. It wasn't in this room.

"There was an accident!" Casper shouted back. "I need help!"

"Go to the hospital," Isla said, though part of her wanted to open the door and see what was wrong. "Or the police!"

"Please, Isla," Casper's voice lowered, then there was a thump sound and a splash.

Looking through the curtain again, Isla no longer saw Casper standing. His body was lying face up in the mud, and rain was coming down harder. A flash of lightning lit up the backyard, and Isla felt the knife in her hand shaking.

"Fuck, fuck, fuck," Isla said, unlocking the back door and opening it.

Holding the knife in front of her, Isla poked Casper in the chest. His face was covered in dark shadows and something red. His eyes were closed.

"What's wrong?" Isla asked.

"Fire," the words came out as a hoarse whisper. "I swam... it hurts."

Taking a deep breath, Isla dropped the knife to the ground and pulled Casper up to his feet. He seemed to be trying to stand on his own, but his balance was off and he looked to be partially conscious. Isla half-carried him through the front door and set him in a chair by the table. In the bright indoor lights, Isla could see fully what was wrong.

Casper was wearing a pair of sweatpants and a thick sweater, but there were irregular holes and scorch marks all over the fabric. The skin that showed through these holes had dark marks, red blisters raised on his skin. His face and neck showed the same marks, and there was a long cut along his jawline. His hair was wet, sticking up in every direction. He was barefoot, and when Isla caught a glimpse of his soles, he saw they were caked in mud and cuts.

"What happened?" Isla asked, locking the back door. "How bad are you hurt?"

"I'm just tired," Casper said, leaning back against the chair and resting his arm on the table. "I'll be alright, just need..."

The man began coughing violently.

"Let me get the first aid kit," Isla said, going to one of the kitchen cabinets. She pulled out the white and red box and set it on the table.

"Can I have some water?" Casper asked, his throat sounded raw.

Silent, Isla filled up a glass of water and handed it to him. After he gulped the water, Isla reached for the hem of the sweater and pulled it up over his head. As he sat shirtless in front of her, she tried not gawking at the bruises, cuts, and burns all over his skin.

"What the hell happened, Casper?" she asked, looking him in the eye.

"I can't," he said, his eyelids drooping, "Later, please."

Isla took the glass from his shaking grip and set it on the table. Then she took his face between her hands, forcing him to look her in the face. "Casper, you tell me, or I'm calling the police."

Forcing his eyes open, Casper focused on her. "Someone... lit Bill's boat on fire."

A list of emotions and questions burned inside Isla's chest. "Where's Bill?"

"I think..." Casper lowered his gaze, "I don't think he made it."

Letting go of Casper's face, Isla took a step back. Old, locked-up memories of Bill kissing Isla's knuckles, forehead, temple, shoulder, etc., rushed through her mind. She felt nauseous.

"I'm sorry," Casper said, then began coughing again.

Wordless, Isla pulled alcohol swabs out of the first aid kit and began treating Casper's wounds.

"I was on a diving trip," Casper explained, wincing at the sting of the treatment, "There were two other divers. We were sleeping..."

He paused to take in a deep breath. Isla wondered if there was any internal bleeding, any concussions, but he seemed alert, just exhausted.

"We were sleeping," Casper continued as Isla covered some of the injuries with gauze. "And I woke up to smoke. The boat was on fire. Bill was in his bed. I ran across the hall to get the other divers, but their door was locked and they weren't answering. I went up to the main deck. The stairs... they were on fire."

Looking back at his feet, Isla could see red blisters on the side of his heels and toes.

"I thought I saw someone lying by the helm," Casper's words became quiet, his tone solemn and shaky. "I-I couldn't see. There was so much smoke. It hurt to breathe. It hurt my eyes. It was dark, too."

"There was no rescue boat?" Isla asked, trying to keep herself from crying.

"There was a boat," Casper said, sounding more firm. "I think it was whoever set the fire."

"Set the fire?" Isla's hands froze while she was pressing the gauze to his skin. "I thought you said it was an accident."

She met his gaze, and she saw the fierceness in his eyes.

"So you swam to shore?" Isla continued, finishing the gauze and stepping back. "How far was it?"

"I could see the town lights," Casper said, running his hand over the gauze on his chest. "When I jumped into the water. It was so cold."

Grabbing one of the folded flannels, Isla wrapped it around Casper's body. She grabbed two more blankets to wrap him up in, mentally kicking herself for not doing this early. If he doesn't die of the burns and cuts, he could die from hypothermia.

"Take your pants off," she said, waiting for him while holding another blanket.

He looked as if he was about to refuse, but then he stood up and listened. Isla looked away as she wrapped the blanket around his hips. When he settled back into the chair, she pulled another seat over.

"Let me look at your feet," she said, and he rested both on the chair in front of him.

"Thank you, Isla," Casper whispered as she treated the burns.

Glancing at his face, she saw him watching her with eyelids half-closed. His eyes looked blurry, not from tears but from trauma. He must be more shocked and confused than she was.

"What do you expect me to do?" she said, meaning the words to sound humorous but they came out harsh. "You show up at my back door, burned and bruised. You don't want me to call the police or an ambulance. I'm shit at first aid. It's not my fault if you die from infection or something else."

A wheezing noise came from Casper's chest, and Isla looked up to see him laughing. It looked painful but he did it anyway.

"Will you tell me everything when you feel better?" Isla asked, spreading antibiotic ointment on the burns.

"Maybe," Casper said, still smiling.

"For payment of my services?" Isla applied a bit more pressure to one of the burns, causing the man to wince.

"Well," Casper pulled his foot away from her finger, "You still haven't given me my refund."

Rolling her eyes, Isla took his foot and wrapped it in gauze. "You can't expect to come here like this, tell me Bill is dead, and not tell me why."

"What makes you think I know more?"

"You don't want the authorities involved."

"Right."

They stared at each other in silence for a moment. Isla tried reading his expression, though it looked like he was trying to not smile again.

"You can sleep on the couch," Isla stood from her crouch and put the first aid kit away. "There's more blankets in the living room."

"Isla, wait," Casper said as Isla stepped to the back room.

"What?" she whipped her head around.

"Don't tell anyone about this, please."

Since Casper arrived tonight, Isla's body had been shaking. She wanted to cry, shout, punch the wall, break a glass. She wanted to hug Casper, kiss his face and tell him she's ecstatic that he is safe now. She wanted to slap him across the same face and demand answers. Now, she was angry.

"Does it look like I will?" Isla grabbed the basket of folded flannels and walked to the doorway, looking at Casper. "This may surprise you, but I care about you, Casper. Maybe as much as you care about me."

Casper's face grew blank, realization setting in.

"You don't have to tell me what the hell you're doing in Scotland," Isla said, trying to mask the shaking in her voice. "I know you're not a scientist, but you don't have to be honest with me. But you can trust me."

"Isla—"

"I need to think," Isla walked to the hallway but turned to look at him again. She scanned his damaged body from head to toe before meeting his gaze. "I'll make dinner in an hour."

She went up the stairs adn to her room. She locked the door, not because she was scared of the man in her kitchen, but she needed the physical act of closing off the world so she could process the recent news and events.

Bill is dead.

Isla placed the laundry basket on the floor and paced the length of her room.

Casper is hurt. Someone tried hurting Casper. He is doing something illegal, or... something that he doesn't want to draw attention to. Something that relates to his scuba diving. I knew he wasn't a real researcher.

Pausing her feet at the foot of her bed, Isla ran her fingers through her hair. She pulled her hair up into a messy bun and rested her hands on her hips.

I don't care. I care about him. I care about this man, and I want to help me.

Chapter 38 - Casper

Casper's whole body hurt, though the pain he felt the most was in his chest. It wasn't an unpleasant ache but more of an epiphany, a realization, a hope. Isla had feelings for him, something that extended beyond a drunken kiss.

When Casper swam to shore, he hadn't known where he could go. If he hadn't been already banged up from the fire and swimming, he would've kicked himself. He *knew* he saw Liam outside the coffee shop, but he forced himself to believe it was just a figment of his imagination. Liam being here, in Scotland, in this town, would mean he either had a copy of Bella's notes, or he was able to figure the treasure's geographic location out through his own research. He *was* on Bella's research team, so had the same level of skills and expertise. But he was here, which meant this secret mission just became very dangerous.

Bill died. Adara and Cyrus also died. From what Isla told him while she was drunk, about her father and his research, and her house getting broken into, meant Isla was in harm's way. Casper wasn't going to let her get hurt, but...

He found the treasure.

Since Isla left the kitchen, Casper had barely moved from his seat in the chair. His legs were still propped up as he didn't want to put pressure on his feet. The glass on the table was empty, and he was thirsty. But he didn't want to bother the woman as she needed time to process all the shit he just dropped on her shoulders.

Carefully, Casper set his bandaged feet on the cold floor. He sucked in a breath as pain etched up his soles and into his ankles, but he carried the glass to the sink and filled it with water. Then he grabbed a bowl and a box of cereal, and returned to the table. He ate half the contents in the bowl before sitting back, relaxing against the chair again.

He could trust Isla, he knew this. That's why he came here in the first place, because something in his gut told him she would help him. His secret was safe with her, even if she was pissed about it. He underestimated her, and now felt bad about all his judgemental thoughts against her. He wondered if she thought poorly of him, thought of him as a stupid, smug American who takes what he wants and doesn't care who gets hurt.

That's what I am, right?

Casper was conflicted, knowing he needed to let the treasure go. He almost *died*, but he needed to return to the dive sight and dig it out. For Bella.

What about for Isla, though?

Finishing the bowl of cereal, Casper could hear floorboards creaking through the ceiling. It sounded like something walking back and forth in a small space. Isla must be wearing a hole into the floor. After some time, the floorboards shifted to the stairs, and Isla came down the hallway and into the kitchen. Her eyes were red, not from tears it seemed but from rubbing them. There was a spot in her hair that looked teased up, as if she had been playing with that section of hair while pacing.

"I'm making chicken and broccoli," Isla announced, her voice showing no emotion.

Casper nodded, unsure of how to respond. She went to the refrigerator and pulled ingredients out, and pulled a pan out from the cabinets.

"I'm a treasure hunter," Casper said. Once he said the words out loud, he felt like laughing at how ridiculous it sounded.

Isla's meal preparations didn't pause, and she said nothing in response.

"My sister was one, too," Casper continued, watching her shoulders tense a little. "She would find long lost gold and jewellery from pirates, but only in the Americas, you know. She worked for museums, at first, but then private contractors hired her."

He watched as Isla placed cubed chicken on the pan and began frying it in butter.

"She was working with a team in Barbados," Casper said, "And she was murdered. No one knows who did it, but I'm pretty sure it was the man she was working with. Liam Martinez. There must have been some dispute over the research, or the pay. I don't know. But... he's here."

"What does this have to do with you?" Isla asked, not facing him.

"I found Bella's notes," Casper explained, "And I wanted to know what she was working on that got her killed. It led me here."

"There's treasure here?" Isla finally turned and looked at him, and there was a curious spark in her eyes. "In the Firth?"

Casper took a deep breath. "Yes."

Isla looked away, her expression showing a cluster of thoughts.

"I think Liam is the one who started the fire," Casper said, "And I think he's the one who broke into your house."

"What?" Isla raised her voice, not in anger but shock. "Why?"

Before Casper could answer, though, her eyes shot up to look toward the hallway and she dropped the wooden spoon she had used to stir the food. Without words, she darted out of the room.

"Isla?" Casper got to his feet and, painfully, hobbled down the hallway. He found Isla standing in a small study, where a stack of books and papers sat on the desk. "What's wrong?"

"They're gone," Isla was thumbing through the documents on the desk, her fingers frantic. "The letters."

"What do you mean?"

Isla stood up straight and faced Casper. "Okay, so, you're right."

"Right about...?" Now Casper was the confused one.

"My father was working on something before he died," Isla said, tapping the top of the book stack. "I don't know what, or at least until now."

"You mentioned something about your father's research," Casper said, "When you were, you know..."

"Shit faced? Yeah," Isla laughed, apparently too focused to appear embarrassed. "He had hidden a plastic bag of letters on the Eimear, and there was a note to me advising me not to tell anyone. Not to trust anyone."

Isla met Casper's eyes, and a silent message seemed to pass between them: *You're no longer "anyone", now.*

"He was looking into Logan's ancestry," Isla continued, "I still don't know why. But here—" she waved her hand at the stack of books and papers on the desk "—there are all sorts of records relating to piracy and oceanographic data."

"Relating to the late 1700s?" Casper stepped closer to the desk and looked at the first page on top.

"Yes," Isla sounded breathless, as if she couldn't believe the connection.

The first page was a copy of a list of dredging records, and Casper recognized the notes from Bella's notebook. His sister must have found this record and wrote the data down.

"Do you think your father was searching for the treasure?" Casper asked, pulling the chair out and sitting down. He tried not to let out a sigh of relief from his feet.

"I don't know," Isla shrugged, "There's no notebook where he wrote down his goal. But the letters were here, on this desk, before we left for the last dive trip. I didn't realize they were gone until now."

"Liam must have taken them," Casper pressed his palm to his forehead, resting his elbow on the desktop. "Do you think it would lead him to the treasure?"

"I don't think so," Isla shook her head, then looked at his face. "How did you know where to dive?"

Casper was quiet for a moment, then he ran his palm across the rest of his face. "My sister's notebook. She had done a full investigation of geographic locations, historical currents, that she had—"

"The GPS coordinates," Isla finished the sentence, understanding growing across her face. "That's why you were so specific about where you had to dive."

Nodding, Casper looked up at her face. She seemed to be vibrating in an excited energy, an increasing motivation, as the pieces and dots connected in her mind. A web casting out, spread in front of her hazy gaze.

"You found something, didn't you?" Isla's unfocused eyes turned to Casper, suddenly peering into his soul. "The dive when you came up happy."

"I... did," Casper spoke, hesitant, feeling vulnerable. He didn't want to tell her about the box he found during the last dive. "It was a necklace, silver."

Isla's jaw dropped slightly. "It was in my father's notes, the ones taken. He mentioned a silver necklace."

"What else did he say?" Casper's eyebrows furrowed.

Biting her bottom lip, Isla stepped back. She suddenly seemed nervous, as if she no longer wanted to speak.

"Where's the necklace?" Isla asked.

"It's still at Mary's inn," Casper said, standing back to his feet. "Isla, what else do you know?"

"I don't know," Isla turned around and looked out the window, which was dark. A cop car sat out on the curb, far enough away not to notice the two figures peering out through the window. "I-I don't understand."

Placing his hand on Isla's shoulder, Casper felt her flinch from his touch. He felt bad, and let go immediately. She turned back to face him, and he could feel the heat of her body.

"The necklace had been buried behind the house, Casper," Isla's voice wavered, and her eyes were wet. "My father had dug it up. And you found it on the bottom of the sea?"

She seemed to be trying not to hyperventilate, as if this puzzle was beginning to overwhelm her and she would soon burst at the seams. Casper held his hand out to her, offering his support. She stepped closer and pressed her face against his shirt, and wrapped her arms around his torso. He held her in his arms, stroking her hair with his hand.

After a few pleasant moments, Isla stepped out of his hug and gasped. "Shit, the chicken!"

As she ran out of the room, Casper stumbled after her. The chicken was burned, creating a nasty charcoal smell. A thin layer of smoke bumped against the ceiling. Casper opened the back door to let the smoke out as Isla cleaned up the mess.

"I'll order a takeaway," Isla said, setting the pan into the sink and throwing the chicken into the trash bin. "Do you want Chinese or Italian?"

"What do you want?" Casper asked, trying not to cough from the second attack of smoke on his lungs.

Isla turned and smiled at him, then pulled a Chinese food pamphlet off the front of the refrigerator.

Chapter 39 - Kelsey

David did not wait until Kelsey was completely out of the water before running out of the hiding spot. The boy charged through the sand and threw his arms around his father.

"What happened with the ship?" Mateo asked, standing behind the boulders still.

"I don't know," Kelsey pulled his feet through the remaining saltwater and followed David behind the boulders. There was a makeshift camp: a canvas tarp to shield out the sun and a blanket laid out on the sand. Kelsey dropped down on the sand next to the blanket, not wanting to get it wet.

"Did the British know who we were?" Mateo asked, bending over and placing his hands on his knees, as if he were confused by the turn of events. "What we did at the farm?"

"They never reached us," Kelsey explained, "Before the fight started. Someone set off a cannonball."

"Someone... on our crew?" David asked, sounding young for a moment before Kelsey remembered he was still a child.

"Yes," Kelsey laid his back against the sand and closed his eyes, breathing heavy. "We were waiting for the British to reach us, to speak with us, and one of the men fired a cannon. I can't even blame the warship for retaliating."

"No one else survived?" David placed a hand on his father's sore arm. "Ryan?"

"Not that I could tell," Kelsey spoke honestly, finding no benefit in lying to the boy. "There may have been others who swam to a different beach, but there aren't many others nearby."

"Filipe," Mateo said, almost to himself.

Looking up at the first mate, Kelsey raised an eyebrow. "I shouldn't be surprised... what makes you think so?"

"You're thinking it, too," Mateo shrugged, his face contorted with controlled rage. "The hatred he had toward you, especially after your last talk with him. But why would he risk the wrath of the British for petty revenge?"

"Some men are evil," David said, which made both adults turn to the boy in interest. "I read that somewhere, but I don't remember where."

"Well, you're right, David," Mateo grinned, "Though one doesn't need to read to know the truth in yer words."

"I never liked Filipe," David admitted, drawing lines in the sand by Kelsey's side. "He was mean."

"He was," Kelsey sighed and sat up, feeling less winded. "He'll find his own hell soon enough, if he hasn't been delivered yet."

"What's the plan?" Mateo asked, and Kelsey realized he was the one being asked. "Captain?"

"Rest up," Kelsey opened one of the sacks and found a green pear. "We'll take the rowboat out and find a beach that leads us to a road."

That's when Kelsey noticed something shining in David's hands. It was the locket. The boy was rotating the large round piece over and over in between his palms, but his face was gazing at the sand with blurred vision.

"We will persevere," Kelsey reached out and gripped his son's shoulder, who nodded in response. "Let's get some sleep."

"I'm not tired, Da," David gave a toothy smile, as if he too had learned fake reassurance. "You're the one who needs sleep."

"I'll take watch," Mateo laughed at the boy's honesty. "I'll wake you when morning comes."

"Better yet," Kelsey nodded at the sun that was still high in the sky, "Wake me up when the sun sets. We'll travel in the night."

**

The sun had barely set when a shout woke Kelsey up. Small hands were shaking his arm, and he opened his eyes to see David's terrified face.

"He's killing Mateo!" David shouted, tears streaming down his dirty face.

Sitting up, Kelsey grabbed his sword from his belt and jumped to his feet. He ignored the aches in his muscles and ran around the boulder. There, near the surf, were two men. Mateo was lying face up, surrounded by blood that filled the lines of his body. It was unclear where the wound was because there was so much liquid mixing.

Crouching over the first mate was Filipe, who glared down at the dying man. In Filipe's hold was a six-inch dagger, which was buried to the handle in Mateo's gut.

As if possessed, Felipe turned his head in a slow motion to greet Kelsey's presence. The sailor's eyes were red, but Kelsey didn't know if it was from saltwater, rage, or demonic possession.

"How could you run?" Flilipe growled, rising to his full height, which wasn't much. "Captain dies with his ship."

"I'm not going to let myself drown," Kelsey held his sword up toward Filipe, and knew talking wouldn't sway the mad man but wanted to delay a fight so he could plan. "I never left the men until the Stock was destroyed."

"You deserve the hell of the depths," Filipe stepped over Mateo's body and toward Kelsey, "I deserved better than you."

"You never had to stay in my hire, Filipe," Kelsey waved a hand around as he spoke, as if his gesture would explain his point. "That was your choice."

"A choice I'll always regret," Filipe fell into a lazy attack position with his dagger, "What do you regret, Vargas?"

Taking a deep, slow breath, Kelsey kept quiet and watched his opponent's shifting limbs. He had to figure out how Filipe would lunge, what part of Kelsey's body the dagger would fly to, Filipe's weak spot. On the Crooked Stock or at a port, Kelsey never observed Filipe brawling He knew it happened but had never been present. Never desired to watch. Now, he wished he had kept a closer eye on his men so he knew their weaknesses.

"What do you have to say for yourself?" Filipe shouted.

"Nothing I say will help you, Filipe," Kelsey said, waiting for violent initiation. "Even what you want me to say won't ease your pain."

"Stupid fancy ideas," Filipe took three large steps at Kelsey, raising the dagger to the side.

Prepared for the attack, Kelsey raised his sword and effectively blocked the swing. Filipe used his empty fist and punched Kelsey in the torso. Rushing backwards, Kelsey sucked in a breath and kept his sword raised. The punch hurt but the torso was not a weak spot for the captain.

The sailor came at him again with the dagger, but this time sliced through the air vertically. Kelsey brought his sword up, running the blade against the length of Filipe's arm. The man screamed in pain and blood dripped through the dirty sleeve of the blouse. Not finished, Kelsey curved downward, bringing the blade of his sword into the side of Filipe's lower torso.

Kelsey had expected the demon to fall to his knees. Filipe instead fell forward, one arm clutching his torso. The weapon in his grip was directed at Kelsey's abdomen. Seeing the flash of metal, Kelsey jumped back.

There was no space behind the captain as his shoulder and calves met the boulder. The back of his head smacked against the rock, but the worst pain erupted from the left side of his navel. Gritting his teeth, he looked down to see Filipe's dagger sticking half-way out of his stomach. At his feet, Filipe lay in the sand, his chest rising and falling quickly.

Without another thought, Kelsey raised the tip of his sword slightly, then brought it down hard into Filipe's neck. A gurgling noise could be heard, but Kelsey didn't care to listen. He had more important things to be concerned over.

"Da, you're hurt!" David rushed over, eyeing the body in the sand. "Take it out."

"No, David," Kelsey could feel the metal piercing through his guts and muscles, an odd sensation that hurt whenever he tried to breathe or move. "Don't ever take a weapon out until you find a physician. You could bleed out."

"We don't have a healer here," David's voice was high-pitched, a sign of his mental distress.

"We don't," Kelsey rested against the rock, his eyes flickering from his son's face to Laird Thomas's chest, which still sat safely under the canvas tent. He had seen injuries similar to his, and he knew he wasn't going to survive. Not here, in the middle of nowhere. Thoughts of possible ways to live tried entering his mind, but he pushed them away because he didn't want to worry about himself. "David, we need to leave."

"You shouldn't move," David took his father's hand, "It isn't good to move when you're wounded."

"I won't get better here," Kelsey grunted as he pushed away from the boulder. "We need to find another beach, find a healer there."

The boy took a moment to think this logic over. "I'll load the rowboat."

"You'll need my help," Kelsey walked to the chest and reached down to grab one of the handles. "Help me with this."

The pain was enough to make Kelsey pant and sweat, and he had to rest three times before him and David placed the chest in the rowboat. David grabbed the bag of food supplies and dropped it in the middle of the boat.

After two attempts to push the boat into the water alone, David looked on the verge of tears. "I can't do it."

"It's okay, son," Kelsey leaned against the side of the boat and pushed. "Ahhhh!"

With the boat in the water, Kelsey and David climbed in and settled into the seats. Kelsey took up the paddles, one in each hand, and pushed away from the sandy cove.

"I can paddle," David reached out for the wooden boards.

"I know," Kelsey grunted and sighed, his vision blurry. "Later, when I get too tired, you can take over."

"It's getting dark," David looked around at the debris of the Crooked Stock, still floating in pieces on the sea.

"I know, son," Kelsey pursed his lips together, feeling the blood on his shirt drying in the sea breeze. "It is."

Chapter 40 - Isla

After a long night of talking, Isla let Casper sleep on the couch in the living room. He finally had to call it quits when the clock revealed that it was one in the morning. When he settled under the blankets on the couch, his knees curled up so his whole body fit on the seat cushions. Isla almost offered to let him use her father's bed, but she wasn't comfortable with that just yet.

Unable to sleep, Isla busied herself with cleaning the kitchen and wiping the floor of the mud from Casper's arrival. She put a load of laundry in the washer, then went upstairs to her bedroom. Sitting in her bed, she tried reading. Her head found the pillow, and soon she was out cold.

Even in sleep, Isla was terrorized by her thoughts. She dreamed of a faceless hooded figure standing behind her father while he launched the Eimear. Isla was standing on the dock, waving goodbye. Her father waved back, smiling, not noticing the dark threatening entity behind him. Isla tried shouting, but water flooded her throat and she fell to her knees, gagging on saltwater. As she choked, she watched the boat float away, becoming a dot on the calm waves.

There was a knock on her door, waking Isla from her nightmare. She sat up in a cold sweat, and could see bright daylight cast across her bedroom floor.

"Isla?" Casper's quiet, gentle voice called from the hallway.

Still in the clothes from last night, Isla jumped out of bed and ran to the door. She opened it a little to find Casper looking down at her.

"I'm sorry to wake you," he said, rubbing the back of his neck. "It's past noon, though. You said you wanted to go through the papers?"

"Right," Isla shut her eyes and took a deep breath, remembering their conversation last night. "Give me twenty minutes."

"Sure thing," Casper stepped toward the stairs as Isla closed the door.

Grabbing a new set of clothes, Isla went to the bathroom. She needed a shower, so took the time she needed to get rid of the sleep sweat. As the hot water rippled down her skin, she thought about the man waiting downstairs.

Last night, they shared a lot about their pasts. Not everything as it would take years, but they were building a foundation that seemed sturdy and reliable. After the initial shock of learning exactly *who* Casper Shaw was, Isla found that she was resolute with his profession. Obviously, he would have to get a new, safer, job if they were going to have a relationship. But for now, Isla didn't know what they were, and she was unsure how to move forward with him. The best step, she thought, would be to solve this treasure puzzle, since her family was involved.

Sliding her hands down her body, Isla felt heat rise in between her thighs. She cupped her curves, and let her hands fall to where the desire grew.

She wanted him. Perhaps they wouldn't last once they found the treasure, or even if they never find it. She wanted him, though; wanted to feel his firm hands on her curves, run up her legs, ride up against where her hands currently massaged.

There were a few moments last night where Isla expected him to kiss her, as their faces lingered close when they looked over documents. He was still in pain, still had bandages all over his body, but when he smiled at her, there was a spark in his eyes that made her think he wouldn't care. He would just pick her up and pin her against the table, and press his body against hers.

With a gasp, Isla felt the wave of pleasure coarse through her blood. She relaxed into the stream of water, keeping her eyes closed as the droplets fell against her face.

Clean and calm, she went down to the kitchen. Casper was sitting at the table eating a bowl of cereal. A glass of milk rested by his hand.

"You don't put milk in your cereal?" Isla asked, grabbing an empty bowl for herself and pouring the rainbow balls into it.

"I know," Casper rolled his eyes, "It's weird. People make fun of me for it all the time."

"It's not weird," Isla said, pouring milk into her own bowl. "It's different."

"Mhmm," Casper grinned, scooping another spoonful of dry cereal with his spoon.

"When you're done," Isla said, sitting down across from him, "You can get started on the papers in the study. I've already gone through them but we need a whiteboard or something."

"If only I had the notebook," Casper said, sounding sad. "I still have the locket and some other notes at Mary's."

"We should swing by today," Isla said, "Pick them up and bring it here."

"No, no," Casper shook his head, "I can't. Everyone thinks I'm dead, and if I show up, they'll ask me about the Greek couple and Bill. I can't get the police involved yet."

The realization of the situation hit Isla like a brick. "Is it illegal?"

Casper hesitated before answering. "Hunting for treasure, depends on how you do it. How I'm doing it, no. But because murder is involved, it isn't going to look good if I don't go to the police immediately."

"What about me?" Isla asked, her heartbeat speeding up.

"I won't tell them about you," Casper said, reaching across the table to place his hand on top of hers. "I'll say I hid in the hills or in an abandoned shed."

Biting her lip, Isla looked down at his soft fingers. His thumb caressed her wrist, sending shivers along her arm and to her spine. She pulled back, thinking how she shouldn't get involved with someone who is likely to leave suddenly, either from death, arrest, or deportation.

"Who's the treasure from, anyways?" Isla asked, lowering her gaze to her food. "What pirate?"

"Still unsure," Casper said, his throat sounded thick with emotion. "I have, or had, a list of possible names. I saw that your father had some documents on smugglers in the area, so I'll start with that to see if I recognize anyone."

Nodding, Isla filled her mouth with cereal so she wouldn't have to talk. Casper must have caught her drift, for he stood and placed his bowl in the sink, then hobbled down the hall to the study.

Taking her time with the cereal, Isla listened to the distant shuffling of papers. She didn't want to get close to Casper, but at the same time, she wanted to do everything she could to help him with his mission. Her eyes glanced at the phone multiple times, debating on calling the police. What would happen if they found out she was assisting a possible criminal? But, what Casper was doing wasn't illegal. Hiding from a murderous explorer was a safety precaution, right?

Leaving the bowl on the table, Isla went to the study and began sorting through papers with Casper.

"There's a name that keeps popping up," Casper said after ten minutes of silent work. There were three books opened around him, two parchments on top of those books, and a notepad in his lap. "Corazón de Oro."

"Heart..." Isla opened her phone to translate the phrase. "Gold heart? It's Spanish."

"It's the name of a smuggler, not really a pirate," Casper said, tapping his pen on the name, which he circled three times. "There's no knowledge of who the man was, or woman. No real name, no origin."

"Why 'Gold Heart', huh?" Isla changed her sitting position so her legs were cross-legged. "Heart of gold, you think?"

"A kind pirate?" Casper let out a heavy laugh, before coughing.

"But he wasn't a pirate, you said," Isla pointed out, "What did he smuggle?"

"He did a bit of everything," Casper handed her one of the open books and gestured to a paragraph. "It is theorized that he was a merchant and just took advantage of any opportunity he could. The reference says the man bartered from Spain, France, all the up to the northern isles."

"He must be Spanish, right?" Isla asked. "Why not Gaelic if he was from Scotland?"

"It also was a time when the Scottish culture was practically eliminated," Casper ran his hand over a bandage on his arm. "Maybe people didn't know Gaelic after the British enforced rules to squash out the culture. Plaid was illegal, so were weapons held by families."

"Huh," Isla raised an eyebrow. "Where else have you seen this name?"

"It wasn't on my sister's list of possible pirates," Casper said, shaking his head. "So I don't know if it's right."

"You're sister could have incorrect notes," Isla shrugged. "She may have missed these references."

Casper didn't respond,and when Isla glanced up at him, there was a fury in his eyes.

"My sister's never been wrong," He said, sounding offended.

"Uh, okay," Isla narrowed her eyes, trying not to get annoyed by his sudden change in mood. "But this 'Corazón de Oro' may be the guy, looks like it as he was one of the few individuals circulating the Irish Sea in the late eighteenth century. Unless you have a better lead."

The more she spoke, the anger grew in Casper's face.

"Casper," she forced her voice to become more gentle, and she laid her hand on top of his, "I understand what you must be feeling. But we need to put our emotions aside if we want to solve the mystery."

"Isn't that why we are doing this?" Casper's voice broke, almost causing Isla to flinch. "Because of our emotions?"

That's when Casper leaned forward and pressed his lips to hers. In immediate response, Isla lifted her fingers to his face and kissed him back. His hands grabbed her arms and pulled her to his chest, and she straddled his hips.

This was it. She was letting herself do this one thing that would make her happy, no matter the consequences. She wanted him, and after rubbing up against his thigh, she knew he wanted her just as bad.

Isla rolled her hips again, and Casper let out a frustrated groan. He slid one hand onto her hip and pressed her closer, making a soft moan escape her lips. She looked down at his eyes, and saw the desire reflect back up at her.

Then there was a knock on the front door, and reality set in.

Chapter 41 - Casper

As Isla climbed off his lap, Casper forced himself to let go of her. Though he didn't want to stop, he knew whoever was at the door must be someone important. Isla closed the study door as she went out into the hallway, where the front door waited perpendicular. So even though Casper couldn't see who it was, he could hear the conversation clearly.

"Isla?" It sounded like Logan's voice, and it was thick and heavy.

"What's wrong?" Isla asked, her own voice clogged but from different reasons.

"It's Bill," Logan said, "He's dead."

There was a pause before the front door closed, and two sets of footsteps went down the hall and into the kitchen. Casper could hear muffled voices, but from where he hid, the words weren't coherent.

Logan seemed like a kind man. He was pretty much Isla's second dad, from what Isla had told Casper. Still, Casper doubted the old man was on the list of those he could trust. He didn't want to put another person in danger, anyways. It was interesting, though, that Isla's father looked into Logan's ancestry.

Isla had mentioned that all the documents pertaining to Logan's genealogy had been stolen, but she had remembered some of the names and recreated a rough chart linking Logan to a man named David Wallace, who lived in the area in the 1770s. Casper really didn't need to know why Logan or Isla was involved with the treasure, or even who the treasure had belonged to. He knew where it was, and that should only matter. But Casper needed to understand the full story, and how the Muirs and the Wallaces were connected.

As quiet as possible, Casper picked up the papers that he dropped to touch Isla. His pants were tight. Hopefully his body would calm down before Isla returned. He needed to focus on reading as time was tight. Liam may find the treasure and dig it out before Casper could, and that would be the end of his revenge mission.

Casper got through one full page before he heard footsteps coming up the hallway, the front door open, and then close. The door to the study slowly creaked, and Isla slipped in through the small space before closing it again.

"That was Logan," she said. Her eyes and nose were red, and tear streaks stained her face.

"I heard," Casper put the paper down, forgetting about it the instant he saw Isla's face. "Are you okay?"

"I had to pretend that I didn't know," Isla ran her sweater sleeve under her eyes, kneeling down on the floor next to Casper. "I'll be okay. Just sucks, you know?"

"I know," Casper placed his hand on her arm and gave her a little squeeze. "I'm here, if you want to talk."

She looked him in the eye, then said, "Thank you," before kissing him. So much for staying focused.

There were so many things Casper wanted to do. He wanted to push her flat on her back, crawl down and pull her pants off. He wanted to kiss her, nibble her thighs, lick her and make her scream. He also wanted to pick her up and take her upstairs. Instead, he let her take control.

She pushed her hands against his chest so he was lying face up. His abs hurt as he rolled down to the floor, and he let out a pained laugh. Isla grinned but said nothing as she swung her leg over, straddling him like before. Through the thin sweatpants he borrowed, and the leggings she wore, Casper could feel the heat and moisture between her legs. He placed his hand against her neck and brushed a dark curl away from her skin.

Placing her hands on his chest, Isla rubbed against him. He was hard and it almost hurt, how bad he wanted her. With his free hand, he wrapped his fingers around one of hers on his chest, and closed his eyes. Her fingers were rough, but the back of her hand and her wrist were soft and warm.

Casper felt her lips against his, and he wrapped both his arms around her. Her tongue pressed against his lips, and he didn't hesitate to open his mouth for her. He let a heavy breath escape his mouth, his whole body concentrating on this mind-numbing kiss and youthful dry humping. Ten years younger, and he could climax from just what she was doing.

Abandoning his mouth, Isla sat up. Casper watched as she pulled her shirt up over her head and tossed it to the side. She hadn't been wearing a bra, so her breasts were free to the cold air and to Casper's sight. Slowly, he slid his palm and fingers up along her belly, in between her breasts. He could feel a shiver spread through her body, and when he cupped her left breast, she let out a throaty sigh.

Her eyes fluttered and her head tilted back, rolled to the side, then she looked down at him. She looked like nothing else Casper had seen before. She was Isla Muir, but was much more. She was everything he desired, everything he cared for, everything he—

She pressed his shirt up and helped him pull it over his head and off his limbs. Her lips went to the chest on his chest, and made gentle bites along his collarbone. Careful of his bruises and cuts, her mouth trailed down to his navel. Her hand rested on the hard spot rising against his pants, and she massaged it.

This time, Casper shut his eyes and breathed a moan. It had been a long time since someone else had touched him, and he forgot how amazing it felt.

Cold air rushed around his naked thighs as Isla pulled the sweatpants off him. He glanced down to see Isla standing up to shimmy her leggings down, along with a pair of dark blue cotton panties. Propping himself up on his elbows, Casper gazed at her feminine beauty, unable to say anything.

"I take it you aren't a virgin, right?" Isla said, grinning.

"No," Casper said, sounding breathless. "But it has been a while."

"Same," Isla straddled him again, and he almost groaned at how close he was to entering her.

Without any warning, she took the base of his cock in one hand and lowered herself down. Out of surprise and pleasure, Casper grabbed both of her thighs tight in his hands and groaned. Her mouth opened wide but no sound came out. She paused when he was inside halfway, then pushed him in completely.

"Oh, my God," Casper whispered, squeezing his eyes before looking up at her. She had a determined expression, with speckles of lust and pleasure.

She placed her hands on either side of Casper's head and looked him in the eye, then began raising and lowering her hips. She rode his full length, almost making him pop out each time. His tip was hyper-sensitive, and he couldn't let go of her hips for he felt he would lose himself in the intensity.

Then Isla started moaning.

It was a quiet, small sound emanating from her throat. Her pace was slow, agonizing, as if she wanted to make this last for hours. Every few minutes she would stop, taking his entire shaft inside her and squeeze her muscles. This would make Casper gasp, which made her grin like she just accomplished something.

Isla was also creating a maddening rise of sexual frustration for Casper. She quickened her pace, and he would feel the rise of his orgasm. His body would start twitching, preparing for the release. But then she would slow down right before he came, and she would lay her upper body against his chest and kiss him deeply. While he enjoyed her playing with him, he couldn't take it any longer after the fourth time.

As her hips began slowing, Casper moved his hands from her hips. One on her upper back and the other on one of her butt cheeks. Then he held her to his body as he turned to the side. She made a strange squeal as he pushed her so her back was against the floor. She reached one hand up and pressed it against his chest, and the other found its way to the little nub between her legs.

The scrapes on Casper's legs rubbed against the rug on the floor, but he didn't care. He pressed his hands flat against the floor so they were on either side of Isla's head. He gazed down at her, and she watched his face as he began thrusting.

Her moan became louder, which seemed to make Casper even more hard. She pulled her knees up, which deepened his thrusts inside her. Her heels pressed against his butt cheeks, driving him in deep into her core.

He didn't want it to stop, but he wanted to come. He could feel the tension rising inside him.

"Fuck!" Isla shouted, and her back arched up towards him. The walls that had been massaging Casper's cock began pulsing, which brought him closer to the edge. He lowered his lips to one of her nipples and sucked on it, causing a tremor to run through her body.

The tremor seemed to set off Casper's climax, and he picked his head up so he could see her face as he orgasmed. His body stilled, and he could feel himself unloading into Isla. Pleasure filled his mind and limbs, and none of the pain in his body existed.

He pressed his lips against Isla, who wrapped her arms around his torso. After two more slow, gentle kisses, Isla pulled back and smiled at him.

"Do you think we could do that again later?" She asked, her face flush from the activity.

"I really hope so," Casper kissed her forehead and rolled onto his side, sliding out of her.

Isla glanced around the room and sighed. "I guess we should do some more reading before then, huh?"

Chapter 42 - Isla

"I know where the treasure is."

Isla had finished pulling her sweater over her head when Casper spoke. He was standing behind her, fully clothed, and his gentle gaze rested on her face. She froze as the words registered in her mind, the fuzzy happy feelings from their physical connection fading.

"Did you connect the dots?" Isla asked, glancing down at the papers on the floor. "What information did you find?"

"No, no," Casper took her hands in his and brought her close to his chest, and she could feel his breath on her forehead. "I wasn't upfront about what I had found while diving."

"You lied?" Isla asked, trying to figure out if she should be angry or not.

"Not really," Casper let go of her hands and stepped to the side. "On my last dive, with Bill, I found a box in the sand. It needs to be dug out, and a chain to help pull it out of the water once it reaches the surface."

"Why didn't you tell me before?" Isla asked. "Why now?"

"I trust you," he shrugged, a small helpless grin on his lips. "After... that—" he gestured to the floor where their limbs had been intertwined minutes before "—I guess I don't have any reason to hold back."

"You trust everyone you have sex with?" Isla blushed, giving a dry laugh.

"I just meant that..." Casper seemed to be having a difficult time speaking, his mouth opening before closing again. "I've been doing this investigation by myself for months, with the research back home and then planning this trip out. I haven't talked with anyone about it, haven't divulged my theories and concerns. I'm really excited that I can share this with someone, especially someone I care about, but it's still hard."

"To open up," Isla nodded, understanding. "Then I guess we don't need all this, huh?"

She picked up the papers off the floor and piled them onto the desktop.

"We should still piece together the facts," Casper placed his hand on her wrist, and she looked up at him, wanting to rest her head against his chest but not wanting to cause further distractions. "We still don't know why your father was involved, or Logan."

"Maybe they were treasure hunters, too," Isla grinned, raising an eyebrow. "They're way better at keeping it secret than you are."

Casper smiled and kissed her on the forehead. "Have you talked to Logan about his ancestry?"

"Not yet," Isla pulled out the chart she had sketched and tapped on the name *David Wallace*. "We need to figure out who this man is."

Casper was silent as he stared down at the chart. "You don't think David *Wallace* was the pirate, do you?"

"No," Isla scratched her jaw, "Unless he changed his name. This family is listed in the town's records before the late 1700s. And I'm pretty sure we would know if there was a smuggler living in our midst."

"Unless everyone stayed quiet about it," Casper leaned against the desk and unwrapped a bandage on his arm. "To keep it secret from the British."

"This is mad," Isla sighed, rubbing her temples. She looked at the dirty bandage in Casper's hand. "You should get cleaned up. There's fresh bandages under the sink."

"What are you doing?"

"Well," Isla was writing a list, items they would need for the trip back onto the water. "We have to get the treasure, don't we? I'm going out to get supplies."

She felt the pressure of his lips on her hair, and he let go of her waist.

"There's a spark in your eye," he lowered his voice, cupping her cheek, "That my sister had, when she was searching for an object. I miss seeing that look."

"Didn't you know," Isla grinned, placing her phone on the desk so she could take Casper's face between her hands, "That you have that very same spark. It's what drew me to you at first. Even if the nudibranchs were a lie."

She kissed him deeply on the lips, before stepping back.

"Where's the next dive shop?" Casper asked, skirting around the fact that Billy Bob's Dive Shop would be out of business.

"It's thirty minutes north," Isla said, tapping the pen to the notepad, "My boat is already stocked with food, and we won't be out for long since we won't have to search for the location. What kind of digging tools do you think you need?"

"A trowel would work," Casper stared at the wall while speaking, his eyes glazed over, "You have chains onboard, right? To lift it?"

"Yes, the ones I have should do fine," Isla finished writing the list and folded the paper in half.

"Do you have a gun?" Casper asked, his voice grim.

"A gun?" Isla raised an eyebrow, confused, but then thought of the mysterious man trying who was trying to kill Casper, and possibly Isla, too. "No, my mother never liked them in the house, so my father didn't keep one. I have two flare guns on the boat."

"It might be enough to scare him off," Casper said, speaking as if he had a personal connection to Liam Hernandez. Well, he did, in a way. "And if you get the flare in his face, it can distract him while you get away."

"I have knives on board," Isla put the slip of paper in her pocket, trying not to show her trembling hands. "And I can defend myself pretty well."

Despite Isla's attempt to comfort him, Casper didn't look convinced. Wrinkles creased along his forehead and cheeks, and his jaw was set, his teeth probably clenched together. Isla pulled him into her arms again and kissed him.

"I'll be okay," she whispered, "We have to do this. Soon."

Nodding, Casper pressed his forehead to hers and closed his eyes.

"I'll be back in an hour or so," Isla kissed his cheek before walking to the door of the study. "Wash up and eat. You know where the extra clothes are."

As she walked out of the house, she locked the front door as if she was the only one living there. Then she turned toward her driveway, giving the officer in the cop car a polite wave as she walked to her pickup truck.

Chapter 43 - Casper

Casper thought he would enjoy being back on the water, but the second the Eimear disconnected with the dock, and the connection to land was gone, he could only feel the heavy beating of his heart. His chest was tight, and his neck and arms itched. The captain of the Eimear, now his lover, was excited about the trip, though.

Isla obviously understood the severity of the situation, but to Casper, she seemed to not understand how dangerous Liam could be. Sure, Bill died. The death of her father may have been related to Liam. But they had been separate from her experiences, and she hadn't witnessed such trauma before. At least, nothing that Casper knew about.

Right before the sun rose above the mountains in the east, Isla and Casper loaded the Eimear with the diving equipment. Since Logan trusted Isla like his own daughter, Isla had a set of keys to access the parking lot before the old man arrived for duty. Before they left the dock, Isla wrote a small note to Logan just saying she was going to spend the next two days at sea. Once all items were snug and safely stored, Isla untied the boat, lifted the anchor, and started the engine.

The drive to the spot would take about an hour and a half. By the time the sun was sparkling down behind the boat, Isla slowed the vehicle down. Casper didn't waste time, and was already suited up in the new rental gear when the boat came to a complete stop. Attached to the various hooks on his belt were a trowel and a chain net attached to a flagged buoy. He knew it was risky showing his location to the surface, but Isla needed to know where he was while he was under the surface.

"Are you ready?" Isla asked, her voice gentle. She pressed her hands against the front of his suit, her fingers searching for any air pockets or tears.

"Yeah," Casper grinned, pulling in a shaky breath through his lips. "Keep a lookout for any other divers or boats."

"I will," Isla looked over her shoulder, like she expected a sea monster to jump over the side. "Be careful, Casper. But be quick."

He responded by kissing her on the lips. She pushed her whole body against the front of his, running her hand over the scuba hood covering his hair and scalp.

"I can't wait to get out of this," he murmured as she pulled away.

"I bet," she made a flirty grin before stepping back. "Let's do this."

"Alright," he placed the regulator into his mouth and pulled his goggles over his eyes. "The box should be directly under the boat, but just in case we're off a little, wait ten more minutes."

Isla set the watch on her wrist, and it beeped twice once the timer was set. Casper sat on the edge of the boat and looked her in the eyes.

"Riches and glory?" Casper laughed, trying to make light of the intense, nervous atmosphere.

"Answers," one side of Isla's mouth curled upward.

Allowing gravity to take over his body, Casper tilted backward and crashed through the water. He gave Isla the signal that he was all good, and then let himself float down to the bottom.

The same scene appeared in front of him, though this time there was no searching for the large rock. He had remembered the coordinates on his camera, having memorized it ten times before going to sleep, hours before Bill's boat turned to flames and smoke. After about fifty meters, his light showed the familiar boulder situated on the seafloor. He hovered over the top of it for a few seconds, reading his compass. Then he kicked his fins so he was positioned next to the rock. It took two minutes of searching around the circumference before the strict straight lines of the wooden box appeared below his gaze.

Grabbing the trowel from his belt, Casper deflated his buoyancy compensator a little so he was hovering over the box. His knees touched the sand and rocks of the bottom, and he found this was a comfortable position to work in. Using just his gloved fingers, he dusted the sand off the top of the box, as well as the edges. The layer of loose sand easily floated away, and Casper placed his trowel near the box. He used the pointed end to dig into the sand, pulling the tiny grains away from the object. It took effort, and after five minutes of digging, Casper found himself breathless. He never worked so hard while scuba diving.

Checking his oxygen levels, he sighed a breath of relief. He still had a sufficient amount to keep working. If he needed to return to the boat for a second tank, he was fine with that.

It took another fifteen minutes to push half the sand away from the box. It was noticeably old, even in the harsh glow of the flashlight. Barnacles crusted on the outside, and other tiny marine invertebrates found their home around the organic material. As Casper brushed and dug the box out of the sand, he accidentally scraped these critters off the box, and they drifted away. The clarity of the water in front of him was decreasing the more he worked, the very grit that he distrubed clouding the space between his face and his hands.

Checking his watch, he still had enough time before he had to return, but he worried this would take him longer. He wondered what Isla was doing up on board. Was she worried about him? She seemed to be earlier. Even though they had just confessed their feelings a few days prior, he felt as if they had settled into a stable, trusting relationship. What if she was just faking it? What if she really was just using him to get to the treasure?

With a careful tug, the box popped out of the hole in the sand. Casper held the box, one hand on each side, and stared at it. *I did it.*

Slipping the box into the chain net, Casper could feel the tightness in his chest increase. He should be happy, elated, accomplished. Why was his anxiety getting worse? All he could think about was what would happen when he presented the box to Isla. The aftermath of discovery.

The chain net was secured. Casper began swimming back to the top of the rock, inflating his buoyancy compensator so he could balance comfortably. He swam a little toward where the anchor would be, and found it. He took time with his decompression pauses, contemplating on his new romance, his new finding, and the end of a mission.

Staring in the gradient blue, his thoughts filled his vision. He could stay in Scotland for five more months with the visa from the United Kingdom. Then maybe Isla could join him in the United States. Meet his parents. With the money they could get from the treasure, they wouldn't need to work for years. If ever again. But what would Isla want to do? Would she want to return to her research? She would want a portion of the treasure, obviously. Casper would give her a large portion, *obviously*. But what would she want to do with him? Was yesterday just a stress fuck? It didn't seem like it was. He *hoped* it wasn't just that.

Eventually, the blue sky glittered through the surface waters, and Casper's head rose above it. He could see the side of the boat, and Isla staring down at him with a concerned squint. He filled his buoyancy compensator fully, and swam to the ladder on the side of the boat.

"Did you find it?" Isla called from above, her words muffled through his hood.

Casper didn't say anything as his regulator was still in his mouth, but grabbed the chain connected to the net and held it up above the water. She immediately threw a rope over the side of the boat, and he hooked the rope to the chain. As she pulled the box up over the side of the boat, careful not to bang it against the wall, Casper climbed the ladder and onto the deck.

"Let me help," Isla unbuckled his belt and equipment, and lowered it to the deck floor.

"Thanks," Casper said, breathless, and hurried to the box. Saltwater dripped from the sides, and the wood appeared waterlogged. It *had* been in the water for two and a half centuries. He examined the lock, and tried pulling it open. No matter how rusted the iron was, it held fast and kept its contents secret.

"We need pliers," Isla said from next to him, and started heading to the tool box. "I think I have a—"

She didn't finish her sentence, and for some reason, that scared Casper. He glanced up, and saw her staring out at the water.

"What?" He slowly stepped up to her, and looked to where she was staring.

Only twenty feet away, a boat was siding up next to the Eimear. It was roughly the same size, but had three tall figures on board. Casper recognized one.

"Liam."

Chapter 44 - Isla

So this was what real fear felt like. A shiver tickled along Isla's spine. Goosebumps rose along her neck and arms, and she felt her guts turn to slush. She clutched Casper's wrist, but felt little comfort in his presence. He was nervous, too, though he didn't show it as he stepped around so he was in front of her, almost blocking her view of the approaching boat.

"Get the flare gun," he muttered, his glare not leaving the other boat.

"They could be fishermen," Isla said, though her instincts told her to lift the anchor and start the engine. "We should at least speak with them."

"No," Casper snapped his head so his shadowed eyes stared down at her. "That's *him*. He will kill us."

Taking a deep breath, Isla walked as casually as possible to the helm and opened the emergency box. She pulled the gun out, as well as two flares, and put them in her coat pocket. When she came back out, the boat had sided up next to the Eimear. Waving to the captain, Isla smiled and strolled to the side. She could see the other two men were dressed in scuba diving gear, nothing else. She could barely see their faces.

"Hello!" She called, sensing Casper moving behind her. "How can I help you?"

"We were wondering if you had a working radio we could use," the captain came out of the helm and stood by the side of his boat. There was a note to his voice that felt strange, as if he was masking something. "My radio broke and I need to make a call."

"Don't you have a cell phone?" Isla asked, immediately seeing all the red flags.

"We aren't the cell phone types," he said, gesturing to the two divers. Both stood close to the side of the boat, their muscles tense. They were prepared to move.

"I'm sorry," Isla said, her hand positioned on the flare gun's handle in her coat. "My radio isn't working either. I'm looking to get it fixed once I get back to shore."

Such a stupid excuse. It didn't matter, though. As she finished her lie, Isla saw the two divers leap over the side of their boat, toward her deck. She pulled the flare gun out and pointed it at one of the divers.

"Stop!" She shouted, making them freeze. "Don't move or I'll shoot!"

"It's a flare gun," the captain laughed, pulling out a shiny piece of metal from his one coat pocket. "We don't want to hurt anyone. We just want the box."

Without thinking, Isla shifted her aim at the captain and pulled the trigger. The flare spit out of the barrel and straight at the captain's chest. The firey bullet disappeared for a second, and then the captain began screaming. He fell to his knees, grabbing for the flare that seemed to have embedded into his skin.

"It's burning me!" The captain exclaimed.

Isla heard heavy footsteps next to her, and just as she fumbled to load the second flare, a burly fist knocked against her head. She tumbled to the deck floor, and her face hit the wood. A burst of pain exploded on the side of her face, and she felt lightheaded. She forced herself to focus on snapping the flare gun closed, and swung it around as she tried sitting up.

Casper was fighting one of the divers, and Isla couldn't see if there were weapons involved. It just looked like hand-to-hand combat. The other diver was dragging the wooden box toward the side of the boat.

Isla stood to her feet. Her legs shook, threatening to collapse from underneath her. She used both hands to hold the flare gun, and she aimed it at the diver with the box. She pulled the trigger, and the flare hit the man.

There was no scream as the diver shuffled sideways, as if the force of the bullet sent him in that direction. He had been about to climb over the sides of the boats, but now, he slipped and fell in between the boats. His large body tumbled into the gap, and a large splash could be heard as he hit the water.

"Gah!" Casper's cry rang through Isla's tunnel vision.

Turning to the brawl, she could see the last diver had cut a hole into Casper's bicep. Blood seeped out from between the neoprene fabric and onto the deck. The diver still held the five-inch knife, which had a serrated blade. The sun flashed off the metal, the reflection bouncing into Isla's eyes.

"No!" Isla felt a rage erupted inside her, and her blood warmed even more. She charged forward and, using all her bodyweight, directed her shoulder into the diver's kidney. The force pushed him to the ground, and she fell on top of him. She could hear him gasp in pain, but then something sharp slid over her cheek. Pulling back, she crab-crawled backward.

Casper took advantage of the diver's prone position to grab one of the oxygen tanks and slam it down on top of the diver's head. Isla froze, watching the diver's limbs twitch. The oxygen tank made contact about four times before the limbs stopped moving, and Casper stepped back.

Isla's cheek stung, and when she touched it, she felt liquid on her fingers. She looked and saw blood covering her hand. Seeing this, Casper crossed the few feet to her and knelt down by her side.

"Are you okay?" he asked, looking at the cut.

"I think so," Isla reached up and touched the wound on his shoulder. "What about you?"

"Few stitches and I'll be fine," he looked around, surveying their surroundings. "Where's Liam?"

"The other diver fell into the water," Isla said, pointing to the gap between the boats. "I shot him, too."

"Where's the box?" Casper stood to his full height and his eyes grew wide. "Was he holding it?"

"I think it went over with him," Isla stared at the bloody mess of the diver in front of her. "We need to call the police, Casper."

She looked up at him, and he was staring off at the water's surface. *Is he planning on running?*

"Okay," Casper nodded, turning and facing her. "Tell them everything. This has gone on for too long."

Climbing to her feet, Isla reached out for him and took his arm for support. "What will happen to you?"

"I don't know," he said, pulling her close to his side. "But just know, you did nothing wrong."

"I didn't tell the police you were alive," Isla said, careful not to brush her cheek against his suit.

"Tell them you didn't know I was on Bill's charter," he ran his fingers through her ponytail, then his hand pressed against her upper back. "Just tell them I asked you for the charter service, and don't have any knowledge of Bill's customers."

Nodding, Isla let go of him and went to the helm. She called the authorities, as well as Logan. She told them about Liam Martinez, and the attack. She told them about the treasure, and how they should get archaeologists out to pull it back out of the sea. She told them that she used a flare gun to defend herself from two strangers, and one may have drowned in the water. She told them everything, except her relationship with Casper, and whatever secret history her father had with the treasure.

Hanging up the radio transmitter, Isla stepped out onto the deck and into the sun. The clouds decided to part, and she had to squint to see.

"Here," Casper had been rummaging around on the other boat, and was now hopping over the side back to the Eimear. In his hands was a plastic bag. "Is this what you had?"

Taking the bag, Isla unzipped the top and pulled out some of the documents. "Yes. Help me go through the documents before the Coastguard arrives."

As Coastguardships dotted the horizon, Isla and Casper speed read through the papers, learning more about the Muirs, the Wallaces, and heritage.

Chapter 45 - Kelsey

By the end of the second day, Kelsey Vargas knew he was dying. By the time the deep waters felt dawn, before the light cast the sea in a handful of colors, Kelsey Vargas was no longer alive. The time in between, between the knowledge of his mortality and the loss, was spent on conveying all of life's secrets to his son.

"David," Kelsey propped up against the side of the boat, a hand clutching his bandaged abdomen, "How much food you have there?"

David looked through the sack, holding up something in the dark. Through squinting eyes, Kelsey could only see the sliver of moonlight glinting off the tin of a can.

"Are you hungry?" David asked. "I can't open the cans, but we have biscuits and—"

"No, no," Kesley pulled a slow breath in through his mouth, his lips feeling dry, "I don't want any of the food. It's for you."

"You need some." David said. "Especially water, I can barely make out what you're saying."

"David!" It hurt for him to raise his voice, but as he felt his body spiraling into exhaustion, he also felt panic. "I am not going to make it. I need you to listen."

The boy became still, and the only movement was the swaying of the tiny longboat.

"The box." Kelsey pointed his chin at the chest in between them. "Open it."

David did as he was told, pulling on the lock a few times before it gave way. Kelsey heard the creaking hinges, and tried making out the parallel patterns on the fabric.

"Can you see the colors?" He asked.

"Barely." David was leaning over the chest. "What is this?"

"It's a lot of things." Kesley shifted his foot into a better position, and realized he couldn't feel his toes. "Mostly pride. Memories."

"It's cloth."

"Yes."

"What should I do with it?" The boy's tone grew dark, confirming to Kelsey that he understood the severity of the situation.

"When the sun rises," Kelsey explained, "Memorize the pattern and colors of the fabric. When you see land, lock it back up, and throw it overboard."

"Why not sell it?" David asked.

"It is not to be sold." Kesley used his free hand to wipe sweat off his forehead. "It is not to be found, understand?"

"I-I don't." David's voice quivered, and Kelsey reached out with his hand.

"Come here." Kesley guided his son over to sit beside him. "I've taught you as much as I can, but you still have a lot to learn. You will understand one day, but if you don't, all is well. When you reach land, or if someone finds you, you must not use your real name. You must not mention me, or the crew, or the fabric."

"I know that." David nodded, placing a rag into the saltwater and laying it on his father's forehead. "I'll find a way back home."

"No." Kesley's grip on David's arm tightened. "You must never go back there. It's not safe."

"Then where do I go?"

"You must become someone new," Kesley said, "Like we are used to."

"Won't people recognize your tattoo?" David said, "When we reach land?"

Kelsey looked down at the ink on his arm, though it couldn't see it well in the dark.

"When I no longer breathe," he spoke with his lips close to David's ear, and he could feel his offspring's hair brushing against his cheek, "Say the sailor's prayer for me, and dump my body overboard."

David recoiled from his father before returning to re-wet the rag. The cool water dribbled down Kelsey's face, and he smiled.

"Even though I've raised you," he said, "In this way of life, it was never what I wanted for you. I've been able to keep you from branding, and I want you to stay that way, son."

"I'll do what must be done." David said.

"Good man." Kesley placed his hand on the top of David's head and pulled him in to place his lips against his temple. "The only thing I regret is not savoring yesterday's sunset."

"Da, I will savor every sunset for as long as I can see," David said, "For you. And for if I shall go blind, I will still face the west every evening and feel the sun's warmth leave my face."

Kelsey Vargas died in his son's arms, and those same arms pushed the body over the side of the longboat. The sky and sea was too dark for David to watch the body drift deeper into the waves, but he watched anyway until the first light approached him.

Chapter 46 - Casper

The only punishment Casper received was a misdemeanor and temporary deportation. The investigation by authorities lasted two weeks, where Casper stayed at Mary's bed and breakfast to assist in any questions officers may have had. He couldn't leave town, and he thought it best to not draw any more attention to Isla, so didn't visit her once. At the police station, they spoke briefly in between questioning. They had a cup of coffee on Main Street once. It sucked.

Out of all the events, not seeing Isla was the worst part for Casper. He wanted to hold her in his arms, caress the skin on her face and back. Their relationship had ended as suddenly as it began, like nothing happened. Because that's how it was described to the cops. They were nothing except business partners. Casper didn't know if they were no longer together, or even if they *were* together in the first place. They were intimate, revealed personal truths about themselves, and went through a traumatic experience together. Statuses and labels were figments that didn't matter, not until the authorities finished the investigation and the reporters left Casper alone.

All these thoughts spun around inside Casper's mind as he sat across the table from Isla. They had met for a second time at the coffee shop, and he had been stirring the sugar in his hot coffee for about two minutes too long. Whatever he splashed in the hot liquids were well dissolved by now, and there was less steam rising from the top.

"The genealogist working with the officers," Isla was saying, her own gaze fixed on the small unlit candle in the middle of the table, "Came back with Logan's DNA test. He isn't pure Scottish, or even British. There's a huge portion of DNA from ancestors living on Ibernian Peninsula, confirming that he is the direct descendant of David Wallace. They are still unsure where this David came from, but they think he was a crewmember of the Corazon de Oro, and fled with the treasure after the ship was destroyed by the British."

"That's fascinating," Casper said, monotone, his eyes glazed over. "Does Logan get a say in the artifacts?"

"Not really," Isla shrugged, then took a sip of her coffee. "The tartan belonged to the MacLeods, but the ship belonged to a Spanish merchant originally, so Spain owns it. But since it was found in Scottish waters, the Scottish own it? It's confusing, but since everyone found out that it isn't *actually* treasure, there's less interest."

"Tsk." Casper shook his head and leaned back against the chair. "I'm glad Logan at least got the necklace."

"Yeah," Isla lowered her voice, looking around the busy coffee shop, "I told him not to mention it to anyone. Since it *is* a family heirloom and I don't want museums taking that, too."

Glancing up, Casper found a group of tourists staring at him. They immediately looked away, but once Casper averted his gaze, he could feel the heat of their watching eyes.

"Are you okay, Casper?" Isla asked, reaching across the table for his hands. He pulled back and dropped his stare to his hands.

"I leave tomorrow morning," Casper said, feeling sour in his stomach. "If I don't leave, I'll be arrested."

There was a moment of silence before Isla stood up and grabbed her purse. "Come on."

"Where are we—?"

"Just come on."

Isla led him outside, and they climbed into Isla's pickup truck. Casper examined the storefront of Billy Bob's Dive Shop, and could see a FOR SALE sign in the front window. The lights were off, and it felt empty without all the scuba diving equipment on the window display.

"There's too many people here," Isla said, pulling out of the parking spot. "So many more tourists since the news release."

"Are you going to stay here?" Casper asked, feeling a little hopeful but also anxious.

"No, I don't think so," she turned off of Main Street and toward her house, "I'm selling the house."

Casper's jaw dropped slightly. "It's your family home! You've had that house in your family for centuries."

"I know," she nodded, then grinned. "I can always come back and visit, but I can't live here. It's been great, but there's nothing for me anymore. Mystery's been solved. Father's been buried, and mourned for long enough."

"Can you go back to your salmon research?"

"Yes," she said, nearing her driveway. "But I don't want to do that anymore."

"So....?" Casper resisted reaching for her hand, in case they were being watched.

"I'm going to travel," she said, parking her car in the driveway, her chin set as she spoke. "I'm going to Paris, first."

Casper's heart dropped. He half-expected her to say *America* or something romantically stupid, but he shouldn't have kept his hopes up. She turned the ignition off, turned to face him, and placed her hand on his knee.

"Do you want to come with me?"

Facing her, Casper couldn't help but smile. Her eyes were filled with worry, on the border of embarrassment, but also hope. Anticipation for this new chapter that may or may not happen.

"I don't *have* to go back to the States," he said, taking her hand in his and squeezing gently. "I've never been to Europe. Are you sure you want me to come with you, though? After everything I've put you through?"

Silencing his doubts, Isla leaned forward and pressed her lips against his. He felt his chest swell with happiness, and he felt a little lightheaded.

"Liam was going to come after me even if you stayed in America," she said, her face hovering in front of Casper's, her eyes intent on his.

"You brought me back to reality; back to life, really. We might not work out in the long run, but I sure hope we do because I've never felt more safe in my life. I love you, Casper, and I want to explore the world with you."

Tears brimmed Casper's eyelids, and he tried blinking them back.

"I know I'm being bold," Isla said, pulling her hand back, "But I think it's called for after what we've been through."

Catching her recoiling fingers, Casper pulled her knuckles to his lips. He kissed her skin softly. "I love you, too."

A tear streamed down Isla's cheek, and she threw her arms around Casper's neck. He didn't care if anyone saw as he felt his heart would burst, and his wide smile wouldn't fit on his face.

"Hold on," Casper pulled back, his expression more serious, "What about the Eimear?"

"Oh, that I'll never sell," Isla laughed, opening the driver's side door. "Logan will watch it for me, and I gave him permission to use it."

Casper met Isla at the walkway, and followed her to the front door and inside the house. They immediately went to the kitchen to grab lunch, which consisted of leftovers.

"Did you find out why Logan's necklace was in your backyard?" Casper asked, remembering one of the many questions he had for the Muir/Wallace Secrets.

"Since Muir and the original Wallace were close friends," Isla explained, forking low mein onto a plate, "When David Wallace was *adopted*, they had to hide the necklace from the British because it was obviously Spanish, and no one wanted it stolen. And the Wallace at the time didn't have a yard to hide valuables in, so they gave it to my ancestor to hide."

"And they forgot about it?" Casper shook his head, sighing. "I have so many questions."

"So do I," Isla shrugged, "But not all can be answered. We just have to make educated guesses and use our imagination."

As Isla placed the plate of food in the microwave, Casper slid his hands around her sides and to the front of her waist, and kissed her on the side of the neck.

"I can't wait to travel with you," Isla groaned, placing her hands over his. "If you fly to Paris tomorrow, I'll meet you in three or four days. I just have to wrap everything up here."

Letting a warm breath out, Casper felt her body pressed back against his. "I'll miss you."

Turning around in his arms, she hugged him back and laughed. "Show me how much you'll miss me, since I'm here now."

Casper picked her up and set her on the kitchen counter, and continued to kiss her neck. She laughed, clutching his arms. She was right, Casper thought. Sure, he would have to leave tomorrow. By himself. He would go to a foreign country, and stay there alone. But then she would be with him, and they would experience the new, scary, awkward world together. And it didn't matter. Isla was in his embrace, now. To Casper, she was the sea, the island, the anchor.

Don't miss out!

Visit the website below and you can sign up to receive emails whenever Isabel Glover publishes a new book. There's no charge and no obligation.

https://books2read.com/r/B-A-MBXI-FFPIB

BOOKS 2 READ

Connecting independent readers to independent writers.